Praise for *Shakespeare's Kitchen*

"Sharply perceptive, enchanting and touching. . . . [Segal] explores the nature of community, what it means to be part of a group and how we form that dense, intricately knotted web of human relationships that define who we are and how we live in the world."

—Francine Prose, *People* (4 out of 4 stars)

"Charming . . . Lore Segal is an astute and gentle observer."

—*The New York Times Book Review*

"The whole is clever, original, precise. It is frankly flabbergasting. . . . At the end of the day, *Shakespeare's Kitchen* delivers a pretty hefty emotional wallop, so that it will be remembered, years from now, as much for its keen insights into the human condition as for its masterful wit."

—Beth Kephart, *Chicago Tribune*

"Brilliant distillations of everyday life. . . . Segal's crystalline prose elevates even the most banal workaday details into art."

—*Entertainment Weekly*, Pick of the Week (A)

"Marvelously original."

—Han Ong, *BOMB* magazine

"An exquisite tapestry. . . . The cumulative power of *Shakespeare's Kitchen* lies in Segal's dazzling ability to merge the mundane details of life . . . with the arc of human emotions."

—*The Washington Post Book World*

"Segal is an enchanting storyteller. . . . She compels our attention without ever asking for it. . . . Her oddly telescoping paragraphs are impossible to resist."

—James Marcus, *Los Angeles Times Book Review*

T0153102

Shakespeare's Kitchen

Shakespeare's Kitchen

Stories

LORE SEGAL

THE NEW PRESS

NEW YORK
LONDON

"An Absence of Cousins," "At Whom the Dog Barks," "Fatal Wish," "Leslie's
Shoes" (published under the title "William's Shoes"), "Money, Fame, and
Beautiful Women," "Reverse Bug," and "The Talk in Eliza's Kitchen"
originally appeared, in slightly different form, in *The New Yorker*.

Requests for permission to reproduce selections from this book should be made
through our website: https://thenewpress.com/contact.

Originally published in the United States by The New Press, New York, 2007
This paperback edition published by The New Press, 2008
Distributed by Two Rivers Distribution

ISBN 978-1-59558-346-8 (pbk.)
ISBN 978-1-59558-583-7 (e-book)

LIBRARY OF CONGRESS CATALOGING-IN-PUBLICATION DATA
Segal, Lore Groszmann.
Shakespeare's kitchen: stories / Lore Segal.
p.   cm.
ISBN 978-1-59558-151-8 (hc.)
I. Title.
PS3569.E425S47 2007
813'.54—dc22   2006030107

The New Press publishes books that promote and enrich public discussion and understanding of the issues vital to our democracy and to a more equitable world. These
books are made possible by the enthusiasm of our readers; the support of a committed group of donors, large and small; the collaboration of our many partners in the
independent media and the not-for-profit sector; booksellers, who often hand-sell
New Press books; librarians; and above all by our authors.

www.thenewpress.com

In memory of my mother

and my Uncle Paul

salt of the earth

Contents

Author's Note

The stories in this book take place in a particular situation; they may have a chronology. There is a protagonist, some main characters and a chorus of minor ones, whom you don't always need to tell apart. There is a theme: I was thinking about our need not only for family and sexual love and friendship but for a "set" to belong to: the circle made of friends, acquaintances, and the people one knows.

The immigrant's loss of a circle of blood cousinships is only one example of a modern experience. I once did a poll of the American-born Americans of my acquaintance to see how many of them lived where they grew up. It seemed that only the natives of the northern suburbs of Chicago stayed or returned home. I had moved my own family there for the first two of the fourteen years I taught at the University of Illinois' Circle Campus. My mother, walking between the trim front lawns under a flowering of trees said, "How happy people must be who are happy here." We moved back to Riverside Drive in Manhattan where anyone—transplanted Chicagoan, European, African American, Asian—might become a cousin, and I commuted to Chicago.

I want to translate Göthe's *Wahlverwandschaften* as "elective cousins," the cousins we choose. I was thinking about the sometime-comedy of providing oneself with such a new set. How do we meet people we don't know? How do acquaintances become intimates? And I was thinking of the sadness when we divorce friends and they turn back into acquaintances who are less than strangers because they can never become future intimates.

Novelists think by writing stories. I had a theme in search of a plot—another modern dilemma. I once allowed myself to be persuaded to turn my novel *Her First American* into a film script. The would-be producer plied me with scriptwriting lessons. They were very interesting. They said that in a good plot nothing happens that is not the result of what happened before or the cause of what happens next. I like reading stories like that, but I don't write them because that's not how life happens to me or to the people I know. The mental hunt for happenings and causes produces ever more stories: What if you had a dog who thought ill of you? Imagine a place and time when crime comes out of the dark into broad noon. What if we were forced to hear the sound of torture we know to be happening twenty-four hours a day out of our earshot? Odds and ends: I watched a salesman walk away from the man who had bought his first computer and was asking, What do I do now? And the old chestnuts: What if you love the person who loves you? What if you have ruined a friend? Each story created its own choreography, became fixed in its shape and would not always attach to what happened before and what was going to happen next.

I have known the state of grace in which everything I thought and heard and saw and read and remembered dovetailed into a novel. Here everything dovetailed into these stories.

I'm indebted to Jonathan Baumbach for the book's title and to my Bennington student who explained the ways in which Jimmy could screw up on the computer.

—Lore Segal
New York City
August 2006

An Introduction

MONEY, FAME, AND
BEAUTIFUL WOMEN

Someone must have been saying something nice about Nathan Cohn, for when he walked in the door of the Concordance Institute that fine morning Celie, the receptionist, said, "Listen! Congratulations! Everybody is just tickled pink!"

Nathan said, "Well, thank you, thank you!" missing the moment when it would have been possible to ask, "Why? What did I do?" for here came Barbara, the institute's archivist, down the stairs saying, "Here he is! The man of the hour!" She hugged Nathan and said, "It's a real coup for the institute! Joe says to come up to his office and be congratulated."

"Let me go and get my coffee," said Nathan. "I can't take congratulations on an empty stomach."

Celie said, "Why don't I bring you up a cup? Milk? Sugar?"

"Absolutely not!" said Nathan. "I'll get my own." The institute's style was democratic. It went without saying that the director, the members of the board, founders, fellows present and past—including the Nobel laureate, Winterneet—and the junior people—associates, student interns, administrative and secretarial staff—were on a first-name basis, except that everyone spoke of and to the black cleaning woman as Mrs. Coots.

"Barbara," began Nathan, "listen, what on earth did I . . ." The good plain woman beamed at him and Nathan said, "How on earth did you hear?"

Barbara said, "Celie told me!"

Celie said, "Your wife called. She says, please call her the minute you get in."

"Aha," said Nathan. So that's how the milk got into the coconut.

Now Nathan wished that he had turned around when Nancy came out onto the porch. Somebody must have called while he was walking the garbage round by the garage. As Nathan was getting into the car, the back of his head knew Nancy was on the porch. He could picture her standing there. She spoke his name but Nathan had already turned on the ignition, or took that moment to turn it on, thinking, I can't hear her with the ignition on. At the corner the light was red. There had been that other moment in which Nathan could have, but had not, backed into the Stones' driveway, had not reversed the direction of the car. The light changed and Nathan Cohn drove the ten minutes to Concordance University, parked behind the institute, walked in to be congratulated and made much of.

Nat Cohn was a bulky man with a heavy tread and an enthusiastic growth of very dense, very black beard. At forty-two, Nat was older than the associates, older than some of the younger fellows, the only poet among scholars. Eight years ago, when Winterneet received his Nobel Prize and retired from active participation in the work of the institute, he'd proposed Nathan Cohn. Nat had been Winterneet's student, and his second book of poems happened to have been reviewed that Sunday in the *Times*.

Nat and Nancy had been married three years when they moved to the small university town of Concordance, in Connecticut. They were excited by this good fortune. The institute, one of the oldest of the genus "think tank," was a beneficent organization that paid its members more or less a living wage to read and write and think. Loosely connected with Concordance University, the institute was housed on campus in the first president's rococo residence, which it had long since outgrown.

Nathan walked, that fine morning, down the carpeted hall to applause from Betty Bennet and Jenny Bernstine, who had to make do with desks shoved out of the way under two carved archways. Betty, Joe's executive assistant, confirmed that she, certainly, was tickled pink. Jenny came and kissed Nathan and said, "It's a real shot in the arm for the institute!" Jenny was the wife of Joe Bernstine, one of the two founders; since Teddy, their youngest, had started school she helped Barbara out in the library. Jenny walked Nat into the kitchen.

The little kitchen looked out onto the first president's rose garden grown wild. The great old downstairs kitchen had been turned into a mail and storage room. Acting Director Alpha Stone perched on the corner of the table pouring coffee for herself and Yvette Gordot into the blue-and-white mugs with which Jenny had replaced the cracked and handleless remnant of the first president's Spode. The kitchen was the institute's piazza, the forum where social and intellectual exchange took place, and coffee was always hot if not necessarily good. There was, as often as not, a batch of cookies freshly baked by one of the secretaries or wives.

The little cozy crowd stopped talking and looked very kindly at Nathan. Nathan understood that they had been saying nice things about him. It was a moment in which the heart in Nathan Cohn's chest should have experienced gratification and disseminated it into the bloodstream to be carried throughout the body like a good first wallop of whisky. But Nathan was doubly distracted by the aftertaste of his bad behavior to his wife, and by waiting to know what he was being congratulated for. Nat Cohn was like a man accosted by someone who calls him by his name, asks after his family—someone whose name he has forgotten, whose face he cannot recall having seen before. He was busy keeping himself from getting trapped and alert for clues.

"So when is it going to be?" asked Yvette. Yvette was the institute's economist.

Nat said, "Nobody has told me any details."

"There's the traditional trip up the Hudson on the Crewbergs' yacht. It's supposed to be a charming event. Nancy will like it. You have a tuxedo?"

"Good grief," said Nathan.

"You can rent them," said Jenny. "All you have to buy are the shiny shoes."

Now Professor Alvin Aye walked in and Jenny told him, "Nat's won the Columbia Prize for Poetry!"

I won the Columbia Prize for Poetry! Nathan Cohn said to himself and felt the jolt of satisfaction. It took this form in Nathan Cohn's mind: Sometimes I think I'm good—I'm better than anybody. Now the world is saying it. My friends hear the world say it. Maybe I really *am*? Now the heart in Nathan's chest heaved and rasped in a way that, had the occasion not been pleasant, Nathan might not have recognized as pleasure.

And now Celie came to the door of the kitchen and said, "Your wife's on the phone again."

Nathan picked up his coffee cup and took the elevator up to his office. Nancy's voice said, "What would it have cost you to put your head out the goddamn car window when you heard me calling you?"

Nathan said, "How could I hear you calling me when I had the goddamn ignition on? What did you want?"

"What do I want!" Nancy said. "What could I possibly want? Anyway I called to remind you to pick up a bottle to bring to the Bernstines'. I take it you'd forgotten we're having dinner at the Bernstines."

"Why should you 'take' any such thing?" said Nathan, making a note on the pad before him to cancel the racquetball date he'd made with young Martin Moses. "Any news?" he asked her.

"Nope."

"No calls?" Nathan asked her.

"Why? Are you expecting something?"

That's when Nathan Cohn could have told his wife that he had won the Columbia Prize for Poetry, but Nathan's mouth remained shut that moment and the moment that followed. Then he said, "One never gives up expecting *something*."

"Not me, not any more. Do me a favor and don't be late again," said Nathan's wife.

"Right you are," said Nathan. They both hung up.

When Nathan walked into little Joe Bernstine's office, Joe stood up and came and shook his hand in the most affectionate way. "Sit down, sit down. The institute is going to pick up the tab for the round-trip for both of you, and the hotel. Have yourself a long weekend in New York."

"That's very kind," Nathan said.

"We *are* pleased," Joe said.

"Have you any idea what I went and got this thing *for*? I haven't had a book in three years."

"Not *a* book. This is for your life's work."

"My oeuvre," said Nathan and laughed.

"Ah, yes! Our oeuvres!"

"Oeuvres here, oeuvres there, oeuvres, oeuvres everywhere," said Nathan. They laughed because they were pleased and fond of each other.

"Incidentally," said Nathan, "nobody has actually informed me that I won the damn thing."

Nathan turned into the Bernstines' drive with time to spare, remembered he'd forgotten the bottle, and backed out. He had to drive way the hell into town, and as he drove, he quarreled with Nancy: it was her assumption that he would not remember that had made him forget. He arrived back in a rage.

"Sorry I'm so late," Nathan said to Jenny. Nat could refuse to look, but he could not help seeing his wife standing by the fireplace—slender in black, black-stockinged legs. He was shocked that she was so handsome, but Nancy had always been handsome and, in the beginning, very good to him and—what? And nothing. Nathan Cohn had remained Nathan Cohn.

"Not to worry," Jenny was saying. "Yvette called and will be even later!"

How could anyone be cross with the winner of the Columbia Prize for Poetry? They came and stood around Nat—his hosts, Joe and Jenny Bernstine, Alpha and Alfred Stone, Alvin and Alicia Aye, and Zachariah and Maria Zee. The men embraced and patted Nathan repeatedly on the shoulder and the women who had not been at the institute and had not got to kiss Nathan in the morning did it now.

Nancy's eyes signaled her husband to come to her by the window. "I call you on the phone. You don't think it worth your while to inform me that you won the Columbia Prize for Poetry?"

"I didn't inform you because nobody informed me."

"What are you talking about?"

"Has anybody called at the house to inform you that I've won something?"

"No."

"Nobody called me."

"How come everybody knows something of which you and I have not been informed?"

"Search me," said Nathan. Nathan looked Nancy in the face. He said, "When I walked into this room it came to me that I've forgotten what you look like." An emotion passed over Nancy's face. If she had been going to speak Nathan preempted her. "The reason I have forgotten what you look like is that I avoid looking at you . . ."

"I've noticed," said Nancy.

"Because," went on Nathan, "it is unpleasant to be met with a perennial glare of exasperation."

"Not exasperation. Disappointment."

"Worse. What is nastier for a man than to be on perpetual notice that he is a disappointment!"

"Such a man might undertake to behave differently."

"I'm going," said Nathan, "to behave differently. From here on in I'm not going to let you spoil things. I'm going to enjoy my prize," and he turned and walked away to join in the welcome of Yvette Gordot, who had brought a late edition of the *Times*. Everybody pored over the piece on the Columbia prizes in which the name of the winner of the prize for poetry was misspelled Nathan H. Cones!

"Why do we think this is me?" said Nathan. "Nobody has officially informed me that I've won anything. Maybe it's not my prize at all?"

Yvette read, "'The coveted prize for poetry goes to Nathan H. Cones.' *Is* there a poet name of Nathan H. Cones?"

"Not that anybody's heard of."

"So, there you are! It's you!"

"Of course it is! It's you!" everybody said, and Jenny Bernstine called them in to dinner.

———

Nathan and Nancy Cohn were seated at opposite ends of the table; their friends did not have to notice that they were not speaking or looking at each other. The talk was of prizes.

"They're funny things," Nathan said. "A prize is the world patting you on the back, and your friends patting you for having got patted."

Joe said, "My mother used to buy us children chocolate when we brought a bad report card home, on the principle that we must need cheering up."

"She sounds like a nice woman."

"She was very nice," said Jenny tenderly.

Alicia Aye said, "Everybody needs cheering up sometime," to which nobody knew anything to say so nobody said anything until Nat declared himself very thoroughly cheered by his Columbia Prize. "The promise," he said, and raised his glass, "of money, fame, and the love of beautiful women."

Nancy got into the car beside Nathan. "Nat, I'm happy for you. It's terrific and you deserve it. Shall we have a lovely time in New York?"

Nathan said, "We can't both go. It's too expensive."

"But you'll have the hotel room," said Nancy, "and the round-trip isn't as if it were the West Coast. Doesn't the prize come with some money?"

"Five thousand dollars," said Nathan, "which we're not spending on clothes!"

"I have some money," said Nancy.

Nathan would have preferred his wife to buy the notion that a sensible economy was to keep her home, but he meant to keep Nancy and her disappointments away from this prize of his. "You're not coming to New York."

Nancy was silent. Silently they got out of the car, unlocked the back door in silence. They stood in the kitchen and Nancy said, "Being your wife has been no bowl of cherries, but it's had its compensations. I'm not a poet or a scholar . . ." Here Nat laughed, but Nancy was going to say her say. "Without you I wouldn't be at Concordance, wouldn't have our friends, wouldn't have gone on the junket to the White House. So, if there's any fun going to happen, I'm going to get a piece of it. I'm coming with you."

"I can't stop you from going anywhere you please, but I don't have to talk to you."

"That's true," said his wife, "you don't have to talk to me." After a moment she said, "You are a louse, Nathan."

"True," said Nathan.

Nat put his suitcase in the trunk and shut it. Nancy had to come round the driver's side, open the door, reach across Nat's lap to take the key out of the ignition so that she could unlock the trunk and put her suitcase in. She shut the trunk, got into the passenger seat and handed Nat the keys without a word. Nat took them without a word.

Celie had booked adjacent places for them, but Nat went and sat in an empty seat in the bulkhead. In New York he was among the first passengers to leave the plane and Nancy saw nothing of him in the airport. She took a cab to the hotel. The beds were twin. Nancy hung the evening gown she had borrowed from Jenny Bernstine into the utterly empty closet and lay in a long bath. No bath is as long and luxurious as the bath in a hotel bathroom.

Nancy catapulted into the New York street. Let the heart be breaking, let life's hope of prosperous love be draining drop by drop, Fifty-seventh Street on a clear June day is a turn-on. Nancy Cohn walked down Fifth Avenue with the noon crowd, and the rich old women and the working young women wore their clothes with style that, high or low, had an idea behind it.

———

Nathan's cab set him down amid the noise and to-do at the foot of the gangway to the Crewbergs' yacht, water-lapped, beflagged, garlanded—a floating party. Thousands of little lights swung their gentle halos in the blue air. The bluish air. Grayish-blue air? Smoke blue, except smoky was what it wasn't. Electric-blue air? Poetry's business is to name what the language has not identified and has no ready words for: what's the blue moment that a summer's day holds against the oncoming dark? This festive dark. Every porthole was lit. Nat thought he made out scraps—wraiths—of internal music.

Nathan Cohn joined the end of the queue and set the suitcase he had been lugging all day down on the corn of a stout woman in jeans, who yelped. "Sorry," Nat said. "I'm sorry!"

The stout woman's tall friend said, "That's—what was her name—Lana Turner, is who that is. I thought she was dead?"

"Jesus god," the woman with the corn said, "That looks like—that *is* Redford!"

It came to Nathan that the reason he was getting no closer to the entrance of the gangway, up which moved the evening-dressed people, was that he had got himself ensconced behind the police barrier with the gawkers. Nat picked his suitcase up and said, "I'm supposed to be inside. Sorry."

Nathan set his foot on red carpet wishing he had Nancy's eye here to catch. He felt the gawks on his old mackintosh. A bottle-neck at the entrance gave him a chance to put his suitcase down. Nathan peeled the coat off the rented tux he had got his regrettably heavy person into with maximum—with memorable—difficulty in an undersized stall in the men's toilet at the Forty-second Street library. The young woman with the clipboard was probably pretty when she wasn't so harried. She looked down her roster and up it and back down. She asked Nathan if he had RSVP'd his invitation.

"No," Nathan said, "because I never *got* an invitation."

The girl looked at him. She might be said to be giving him a look which was not pretty.

Nat said, "I'm one of the prizewinners—the prize for poetry. Nathan Cohn."

The girl turned away—looking for a bouncer? This was the fortunate moment when Barret Winburg, an old New York acquaintance of Nat's, stepped on board. Barret, the winner of the prize for fiction, had his name promptly identified in its alphabetical place on the roster and vouched for Nathan Cohn's not only being Nathan Cohn, but being indeed the winner of the prize for poetry. "And long overdue, too," Barret told the girl. "You're looking at a poet as good as the best or better, who might well be *the* poet of our generation."

"Jeez," Nat said, "I just wish I were sure I'm *the* Nathan Cohn."

The girl, relieved, smiled prettily and pointed the two prizewinners toward a table where they must, please, pick up their name tags. Nat had cause to be sorry he hadn't stuck with Barret. He'd asked to be shown to the cloakroom, where he stowed his mackintosh and suitcase. By the time he got to the table, Barret was nowhere in sight. Unwilling to hassle the two smiling, middle-aged volunteers, one in pink, one in silver, he accepted the name tag that read "Nathan H. Cones" and carried it round the corner, where a trio of talented, tuxedoed youngsters from Julliard were playing Mozart. Nat took the card out of its plastic and, using the wall as support, wrote NATHAN COHN on the back, returned it to its holder and pinned it on his lapel.

Nat walked into glamour. Mozart dropped gracefully away before a jazz combo at the foot of a stair. The smallest, blackest of the three musicians exposed his throat and blew a long, high note of unregenerate and seditious joy. Neither the laughing, slender couple, who skittered by, nor the glittering old woman, who passed Nat on the bright stair, looked like writers. The rich people.

Nathan trailed his hand along a gleaming banister of rubbed wood. The brass fittings flashed needle points of light. In a white-and-crimson space he was offered champagne. A waiter put a glass in Nathan's hand. How, if Nancy's name wasn't on the roster, would she make it on board? Where'd Barret got to? The impressive, unsmiling man with his back against the wall had nobody to talk to, either—one of the newer poets Nat hadn't met? Oughtn't two lone poets make common cause against fortune and indifference? Nat took a swallow of his drink, turned to the unsmiling man and said, "Before I moved to Connecticut, I couldn't have walked into a New York party without knowing two-thirds of the guests. Eight years change the scene. Or are these the rich people?"

The man did not smile, but, in response to an infinitesimal beeping, produced a walkie-talkie from behind his back, brought it to his lips, and, speaking low, said, "Not on the roster? What does she say her name is? Hold her there, I'll be right down. Excuse me," he said to Nathan, and made for the stairs.

Nat opened the nearest door into a mauve bathroom. The stool was marble, the lid rosewood. Nat sat on it and sipped his champagne. The flusher was a 14-carat gold dolphin.

Nathan walked down another stairway, looked through a glass wall and there they were—the beautiful women and the famous people—Q and X and Y, and Winterneet. Wasn't that where Nathan was supposed to be? He approached his face to the glass, he knocked on the glass, on the other side of which Winterneet's back was turned to Nathan. Winterneet was talking with two beautiful women, one black on black, one white and gold, and sweet and twenty, both. The black one had eyes so lustrous they looked as if they had been shined to a high gloss with an extra layer of polish. The other one had pale hair cut short and ruler straight, which swung in a single movement with the movement of her head. Her head kept moving on the other side of the glass, on a level with Nathan's eye. Nathan could not hear what Winterneet was saying that made the two young women's mouths open. They laughed with their tongues and their white teeth. Nathan saw, behind the glass, in the far corner, Nancy laughing with Barret Winburg, and here came the young person with the clipboard calling Mr. Nathan H. Cones? "Is Mr. Cones here, please?"

"*Cohn*," said Nathan. "Nathan *Cohn*."

"Dinner is served," the girl said, "and Alice is going to usher you." It was the golden darling who took Nathan's arm. Nathan experienced a small thrill of horror. He thought, I'm not up for this. This needs preparation. Young Alice hurried Nathan along at a smart pace. Nat, galumphing beside her, glimpsed the pure throat, the cheek outlined with a finely furred halo of light. Don't, prayed Nathan Cohn, let me fall in love between here and "*Where*," he asked the girl, "are you taking me?"

"Your table."

"Quick! Tell me what they're going to do to me!"

"They have a prizewinner for every table of twelve. Your hostess is Madame Forage."

"Wait one little old moment," said Nathan. "Is this a fund-raiser, or what?"

"I guess maybe how they pay for the prizes? Each table," the girl spoke backwards as she preceded him up yet another stair, "has got a theme, a color scheme, and a logo. Your hostess is French, so you are red-white-and-blue, and your logo . . ."

"Don't tell me! Wait wait wait wait wait wait! The Eiffel Tower!"

"*Right*!" cried young Alice.

"I'm not sure," worried Nathan, "that there's anything left of my poor old French!"

"She's deaf anyway. But!" said Alice, "on your other side you get to sit next to Betsy Morrowell!"

"I do?" said Nathan. "Who is Betsy Morrowell?"

"Betsy Morrowell!" said Nathan's usher. "You don't know Betsy Morrowell? Don't you watch TV?"

"Never miss my soap opera," Nathan said stoutly.

"And you never saw *Betsy's Bazaar?* It's been around for absolutely ever! I've been watching since I was a child!"

"That long!" said Nathan.

"My mom let me watch with my supper."

"Brief me! What's it about?"

"It's about this woman. Her husband gets sent to I guess some place like Arabia, I guess, as an ambassador or something. Betsy gets bored with ordering servants around, so she sets up a booth in the bazaar and all the things that happen every week with a different tourist."

"I think I . . . I do remember," said Nathan.

They stepped out into a dazzle of flowers and lights and Handel's Water Music. Across the black river on the left moved the lights of New Jersey, and Manhattan's Upper West Side on the right. Alice walked Nathan through a group of mimes. One knelt and bent her charming head over Nathan's hand; one threw a garland of flowers over his shoulders. "Thank you! Thank you!" Nathan said to them. People sitting at a great round table rose at his approach. They applauded. Nathan, who had meant to continue cool and snotty to the end, felt his throat constrict. Out of a centerpiece of red roses grew the Eiffel Tower made of white sweetheart roses and blue ribbon. They seated themselves. The card at Nathan's place read NATHAN H. CONES. "Well, this is very brilliant!" Nathan said to the noble-looking, very old woman on his right. He assisted her liver-spotted, gnarled, beringed hands in the unwrapping of the red-white-and-blue favor. She held it up: a lipstick in the shape of the Eiffel Tower. She pointed to the favor on Nathan's golden plate. He unwrapped a white Eiffel Tower–shaped mechanical pencil with a little lever that could make it write in blue and in red. The large, blond male on madame's other side was shouting French into her ear, and she turned to him.

Nathan was grateful to young Alice. He could imagine himself asking his partner on the left, "Haven't we met somewhere?" She looked familiar. "Did you and I go to Music and Arts together? Kenyon College? Not Kenyon. Have you been to Concordance?" She was a good-looking, bright redheaded woman between twenty-eight and fifty, with powerful jaws and more teeth than ordinary people carry inside their mouths. It was a brave and competent face. Nathan perfectly remembered watching her perform an athletic feat of slapstick. Nat remembered respecting or, remembering, respected the decades of work behind the mastery with which the actress had mugged and delivered her silly lines. Here she sat, next to Nathan, and seemed not to be going to waste her smile on his occasion. Nathan could imagine her life crowded with men and occasions. She had the right to look—irritated was what she looked, though not, probably, with him. Nathan didn't think she was sufficiently conscious of his person to be irritated by it. She appeared to be irritated by her salad, at which she kept poking her fork. Nathan desired to impinge, to become real to Betsy Morrowell. While he busied himself in the formulation of something clever and ever so mildly impertinent with which to startle Betsy Morrowell's attention, his eyes rested on his wife. Nancy sat on the far side of the Eiffel Tower. The man on Nancy's left had turned so completely toward her, his back was turned against the woman in mauve who sat on his other side and looked cross, poor thing, unable to impinge.

Betsy Morrowell suddenly said, "I loathe mimes."

Nathan laughed. "I don't think," he said, "that I have ever met anyone with enough passion on the subject of mimes to *loathe* them!"

"They're elite!" Betsy Morrowell said, showing her teeth.

"Why should *their* being elite bother *you*?" Nathan asked her.

"Mimes!" spat Betsy. "How many people even know mimes even exist?"

"I see! I see! I'll tell you what I see," said Nathan, "and it's sort of wonderful: It bugs you that the few people who know that mimes exist mightn't know that you exist. Just as it bugs me that the masses of people who watch *you* don't know *I* exist!"

Here Betsy Morrowell looked at Nat. "What do you mean?" she said.

Nat saw Alice coming to fetch him and said, "I've got to go get me my prize. Don't let it bug you—it's all of five thousand bucks." Nathan Cohn and Betsy Morrowell looked past each other's eyes and their two smiles curled away from their teeth.

The exchange had not been even. When Betsy Morrowell's manager, in the limousine on the drive home, asked her who she'd sat next to, she frowned and said, "Some man, I think." But the Columbia Prize–winning poet, Nathan Cohn, mentioned to Celie, at the institute on Monday morning, that he'd sat next to that woman on TV—what's her name? Morrowell. He said he hadn't even known who she was. He said it in the kitchen to Joe's assistant, Betty, and again to Mrs. Coots when she came to do out his office. He told Ilka Weisz at the Bernstines' reception for the new director, Leslie Shakespeare, that he had sat next to Betsy Morrowell on the Crewbergs' yacht, and that he hadn't known who she was, and blushed when he remembered that he had told it to her on the Bernstines' porch when she came to be interviewed for the junior appointment at the Concordance Institute.

————

Let Nathan explain and rant and demand to see the manager, the bank would not understand, would not cash, would not allow Nathan Cohn to deposit a check for $5,000 made out to Nathan H. Cones. The manager advised him to return it to the organization and have them issue him a check with his name correctly entered. This Nathan did. He waited a week and a day and then he called. He explained about the check. The girl said, "Let me switch you to Accounts." Accounts had an English voice. "Mixed you up, did we? Oh dear!" She thought she remembered sending this check up to Mr. Block, who was out to lunch, but would call as soon as he got back if Mr. Cones would leave his number.

"Not Cones!" Nathan said. "*Cohn*. I think, maybe *I* better call *him*." Nathan called and explained. Mr. Block said he would look into it, give him till Monday. "I'll even give him till Tuesday!" Nat said to Nancy, but Tuesday he was doing an out-of-town reading, Wednesday he plain forgot, and when he called Thursday, Accounts said, "Fact of the matter is half our files are on the twenty-first floor. We're in the middle of moving and every-thing's a bit of a shambles."

"What's your name, please?" it occurred to Nathan to ask her. It was Joyce. "Well, Joyce, you've been very helpful. Short of getting my money I'm glad to know it's a shambles that's holding it up."

"You give us a week to get ourselves sorted out," said Joyce.

"They're moving to the twenty-first floor," Nathan reported to Nancy.

Nat gave them *two* weeks. Accounts asked him what she could do for him. Nat said, "Could I speak to Mr. Block, please?" Mr. Block was in a meeting, but if he would leave his number, Mr. Block would call as soon as he got out. "Could I speak to Joyce, please?"

"Joyce is no longer with us," said Accounts.

"What is your name?" Nathan asked the girl, and her name was Tracy. Nathan explained to Tracy, who said, "Hold on."

"What's happening?" Nancy asked Nathan.

"I'm holding on," said Nathan.

Tracy came back and said, "We don't have a check for Nathan Cohn. We have a check for Mr. Nathan H. Cones."

"Thanks," said Nathan, "I better speak to Mr. Block."

When Nathan called some minutes before five, Mr. Block had left for the day. The following morning Nathan logged the time, 10:14, when Mr. Block had not yet come in, in the margin of the long poem on which he was then at work. Later he kept a regular notebook logging the day and hour when Mr. Block was lunching with a client; was out sick; had returned but was in conference in the president's office but would call back if Mr. Cones would leave his number.

"CohnCohnCohnCohn," shouted Nathan.

Nathan called Winterneet and asked him if he had heard of a poet name of Nathan H. Cones.

"No," said Winterneet. "Is he any good?"

"I think he won my Columbia Prize," said Nathan.

"Speaking of Columbia Prizes," said Winterneet, "didn't poor Barret Winburg get one the same year as you?"

"Why 'poor' Winburg? Didn't he get *his* five thousand?"

"Dead, isn't he?"

"Dead! Winburg? No way!" Nathan meant, How could Winburg be dead and I not know it! Nathan was tremendously upset.

Winterneet said, "I thought I read an obituary in the *Times* a couple of weeks back, but my memory is like the old gray mare: she ain't what she used to be."

"Nancy, what happened to my old batch of the *Times*?" hollered Nathan.

"Threw them out so you can start a new batch," shouted Nancy.

"Thanks a whole heap!" yelled Nathan. He called a friend on the Book Review and said, "Listen, Winburg didn't die, did he?"

"Not that I know," said the friend. "We ran a review of something of his last Sunday—"

"If the *Times* ran a review of Winburg, he is not dead. Thanks."

After lunching with the president on November 30 at 1:44, Mr. Block suffered a massive heart attack and never regained consciousness.

"Shit. Sorry," said Nathan. "Let me talk with Tracy, please."

Tracy had got married Saturday and had taken time off to go on her honeymoon. "She won't be back till the New Year," said a Southern voice that might or might not be black.

"What is your name?" asked Nathan.

"Miss Martin." Miss Martin said she knew how these mix-ups go. "The longer they go on, the more people get to mess up."

"It's become a sort of fever with Nathan," Nancy told Jenny Bernstine over lunch early in the spring. "He calls on the dot of ten and again at eleven and every hour on the hour."

"I can see how maddening it would be."

"What I'm afraid of," said Nancy, "is they've put him down for a madman."

Fevers burn themselves out. Nathan's rampage passed. He still called, perhaps once a month and tried to explain to the several men and one woman who came and went in Mr. Block's old job. He chatted with the sympathetic Miss Martin, who was thinking of going back to school. Nathan encouraged her.

In the years that followed Nathan Cohn published three books and obtained, if not fame, a degree of eminence among his peers. He got grants of money. He slept with several women—one of them beautiful—mostly, but not always, during the times he and Nancy lived apart. These times grew fewer and briefer. The virulence of their angers and disappointments had not resolved so much as retired. Nathan put on more weight, but his hair remained black. Then he became ill and was very ill for some years, and got better and had ten years in which he did what many thought, and Winterneet said, was his best work. There were blessed months in which the long poem on which he had been stuck for half a decade spun itself out of a place in his head over which he had no say: He played words like a juggler, phrases rhymed in rhythms. Nathan was master of the English tongue—Nat Cohn owned the language in the year before his illness caught up with him.

———

Fast forward. Nat's head lies flat on the white hospital sheet. He is counting the poems he got right—three, four, five in the first book—two in his last. He finished the long poem, but the first line of part three, over which he had that altercation with the editor and had given in, honorably, because he had come to think that she was right, resulted in a skipped beat that continued to trouble Nathan. He persuaded himself again and again that it was all right. Now it twitches his lip.

"Nat?" Nancy leans her face down to him. "What is it?"

"That wasn't my prize," Nathan says.

"Of course it was!" Nancy straightens up. "He never did get his $5,000 made out to the wrong name," she says to Joe Bernstine, who is sitting on the other side of Nat's bed.

"When all he would have had to do was endorse the wrong name." Joe Bernstine looks down sadly.

He is sad for me, thinks Nathan.

Are Nat's teeth smiling between his parted lips? "I wonder . . ."

Nancy and Joe lean down their good faces. "What, Nathan?"

". . . if I was *the* poet."

"Which poet?"

"*The.*" Which is now moot, Nat thinks he is saying but might not be making any sound, might no longer be moving his lips to say mooter, mootest.

Cousins

AN ABSENCE OF COUSINS

Ilka, an only child and a refugee from New York, was always asking people how they had met. "Did you meet here, at the Concordance Institute?" she asked in the silence that gaped after Joe and Jenny Bernstine went inside to get the drinks.

"No. I met Alfred at a sandwich bar during a pilots' strike," said Alpha Stone, the institute's acting director. Ilka had spoken with her on the telephone to make arrangements for this interview. Professor Stone turned out to be small, round and smooth. Her husband was large with a very large, shockingly handsome face—a countenance. Ilka found it hard to look at him and looked away, found it hard not to look and looked at him.

It is always interesting to learn how male and female find each other, but that might not be the information for which Ilka foresaw her most immediate need. "How did all of you meet each other? I mean a new set of friends."

"Everybody went to school with everybody in Chicago," said the child who had opened the front door in order, it had seemed to Ilka, to block it with her body and prevent her from coming in. Ilka had rearranged her face to hide a regret at the young girl's heavy jaw, the unsmiling mouth, and Jenny Bernstine had come and said, "Bethy, go dear. Upstairs, love, and do your homework. Teddy, put the dog out in the yard, please."

Jenny Bernstine brought the visitor into the foyer. "Your plants look so enthusiastic!" chattered Ilka.

"Aren't they ugly!" Jenny Bernstine had shaken her head at so much healthy, undistinguished green life. "Bloom! Bloom! Nothing but bloom!" Her foot inched a little potted purple-flowering bush into a shaft of sunlight. "You kind of wish they'd die so you could throw them out." She frowned at the rubber plant. Its naked stem grew to the ceiling, bent to the right, and ended in three large, highly polished, deeply green leaves. Here came Joe Bernstine, the institute's founder and president, and led Ilka out onto the covered porch where young Bethy reappeared and stationed herself so that Ilka had to look and talk to the right or left of her head, and the child kept her head in motion.

"How did I meet you?" Alpha Stone asked when Jenny came with the ice and the glasses.

"Graduate school in Chicago."

"How did you get talking together?" asked Ilka. "Where?" Ilka saw the hand of the beautiful Alfred caressing the edge of the newspaper that lay on the little table by his elbow and she talked faster: "How did you get to be in the same place?"

"I think Winnie brought you over, no?"

"Yes, I think," said Jenny Bernstine.

Ilka said, "How did you meet Winnie?"

"Leslie picked him up when Winnie's car broke down—Winnie

had gone to pick up—Joe, what was the name of the Kells expert nobody could remember having invited?"

"Or heard of ever again, nor thought of from that day to this."

"That's sad!" said Ilka. "You meet people and afterwards you drop out of each other's head. That's terrible."

"Leslie picked him up and brought him over," said Jenny Bernstine.

"How did you know Leslie? How did Leslie know Winnie?" asked Ilka, and Alfred Stone picked his paper up and began to read it. He was not a member of the set of Chicago friends, who started remembering.

"Winnie married Edwin's sister."

"Dorothy, his half-sister."

"They met at Amherst."

"How?" asked Ilka, but the doorbell was ringing. It was Professor Aye, a huge old man with a massive head of white hair in a state of cheerful revolt. He shook Ilka's hand and said, "Martini please," and Professor Zee, who said, "Don't introduce us. Ilka and I had lunch. Scotch and water. Thanks." Again the bell rang. Joe Bernstine brought the members of the institute onto the porch. Everybody was given a drink while Ilka tried to figure which of them she had met in the course of the day. What was the name of the man with all that black hair, who had been at the breakfast? He was coming over to sit down beside Ilka. He said that in New York, when he got the Columbia Prize for Poetry, they seated him next to that TV actress with more teeth in her mouth than ordinary people. The bank, he added, would not let him deposit his $5,000 check made out to one Nathan *H.* Cone*s*! Here Alpha Stone asked who would be available to meet with Leslie Shakespeare Thursday and what time and Dr. Alfred Stone, who was not connected with the institute, looked at his watch, returned his paper to the little table, and went to sleep.

The discussion of the directorship was a subject on which the junior candidate could have nothing to say. Ilka held her head at the alert but discreet angle of one attending a conversation that was none of her business unless they stopped having it and interviewed her and she got the job, in which case she probably ought not to hear what they were saying. For a while Ilka enjoyed eavesdropping on a world of whose existence she had known nothing until her arrival in Concordance that morning. But it is hard to keep the mind on dates and arrangements concerning one Leslie Shakespeare with whom one had no history, of whom one knew no stories, in whose existence, since she had never checked it out with her own eyes, Ilka did not know that she could not believe.

Ilka searched for something to entertain her. She practiced telling Jenny Bernstine to her New York friends: Around forty. Against the startling whiteness of Jenny Bernstine's hair, the skin showed like deepest summer. What sort of animal did that flat-faced, pug-nosed handsomeness remind one of? Not a cat, not a monkey. A pug. Jenny Bernstine, looking with affectionate anxiety around the party on her porch caught Ilka's eye, got up, came around. She pulled up a chair, reached for Bethy and locked the child between her knees, saying "Search committees!" Jenny Bernstine frowned across the space that separated her from her little, smiling, agile husband who moved among his friends with an air of happiness. Ilka felt at leisure to study, at a remove of inches, the soft topography—lines, mounds, declivities—of Jenny Bernstine's middle-aged cheek, as tender as if the top layer had been taken away to expose the fine-grained second skin. Jenny said, "We can't wait for Leslie to take over the directorship. He's English, you know. They were co-founders, Joe and Leslie. They ran the institute in those first years, as president and director and no one thought which was which. Joe needs to get on with his own work!" Even the conversation of a search committee—at least any one round of it—runs its course and runs out. The silence woke Alfred Stone. Now Professor Zee turned to the candidate whose heart flipped like a fish inside her chest. Professor Zee asked Ilka if she knew that Winterneet had done a lecture series for them at Concordance the year before his Nobel Prize.

"Ah!" said Ilka.

Jenny Bernstine said, "He lives on the other side of town. We'll give Ilka our Concordance tour."

Dr. Alfred Stone looked at his wife and Professor Stone said, "So Thursday is a possibility for everybody?" She got up. Everybody was getting up. At the door the subject of the Thursday meeting with Leslie Shakespeare erupted once more. Alfred Stone beat his thigh with the roll of his newspaper.

Jenny Bernstine drove. Ilka sat beside her and looked where Joe, in the backseat, pointed. "See that white building?"

Ilka saw several white buildings. She saw the walls and corners of more buildings, all of them more or less white. Ilka said, "Aha?"

"That's the Highell Student Center," said Joe. "Over there is the new library that was only finished five years back."

"Ah!" said Ilka.

"Seven," said Jenny. "That was after Leslie left."

"And Winnie got married. You're right!" said Joe. "It was only finished seven years ago."

"Dorothy was not a bad poet in her own right," mused Jenny.

"Which is Dorothy?" asked Ilka.

"Dorothy Highell. Winnie's first wife," said Joe. "Popsicle money. Dorothy used to say her grandfather Highell invented the Popsicle stick. Funds the institute along with some federal dollars."

"Aha!" said Ilka.

"See that little building with the pillars? In 1886 that *was* Concordance College."

"Aw!" said Ilka.

"Now," said Jenny, "we'll give you our Concordance town tour."

"Do you like living in a small town?" asked Ilka, looking hard out of the window. "American streets always look too wide for the houses. I think American houses are always wanting to get away from the houses across the street and go West."

"The bank," said Jenny. The black glass block had been stood down on Main Street, a wandering piece of Madison Avenue. "Now!" said Jenny Bernstine. "Look up the hill to your right— look, look, look. Keep looking . . ."

Ilka saw bushes, bushes, bushes.

"There: Winnie's house," said Jenny.

Ilka thought she might have seen a yellow corner and a lot more bushes.

"Who will I talk to?" Ilka said to her friends in New York and started to cry. Her friends waited for her to finish. Leina, who sat beside Ilka, patted her arm.

Herbert said, "Winterneet lives in Concordance."

Ilka said, "He did them a lecture series the year before his Nobel Prize."

Jules said, "I knew this fellow—his brother-in-law used to play golf with the best friend of Winterneet's lawyer. I'll see if I still have his number."

"This is your chance to discover the real America," Ilka's friends said to her. Ilka was a talker. Her friends were familiar with her refugee anecdotes; the friends of longest standing had seen her through her New York anecdotes, and she had seen them through theirs.

Ilka said, "I've got this theory that refugees don't make discoveries. When discoverers finish discovering they retire home to Lisbon or London. It took me a decade to settle Manhattan and now I'm supposed to discover Concordance!" Ilka started crying again and said, "Bet you there are no refugee discoverers."

"I have a theory," Ilka said to Jacquelyn, "that there are no refugee discoverers, or did I tell you that already?"

"That's all right," said Jacquelyn. "Go on."

Ilka practiced her theory on her friends, and on her circle of acquaintances, and on the circle that surrounded her acquaintances—the people one knew in New York. The thing acquired shape and developed a skin: "It took a decade to find the right drawer to keep my spoons in and turn on the bathroom light without groping and now I'm supposed to emigrate to Concordance! I don't know anybody in Concordance!"

Everybody said, "Winterneet lives in Concordance," and Ilka always said, "He did them a lecture series the year before his Nobel Prize."

Ilka was astonished at the number of people she knew who knew people or knew people who knew people in Concordance, and they wrote down names and numbers for Ilka to call. A man whose name Ilka had forgotten so often she could never again ask him what it was gave her the number of the woman he had dated in Ann Arbor, who would love Ilka, whom Ilka would love. "Tell her I told you to give her a call."

"Can you just give people calls?" asked Ilka.

"You'll come and visit!" Ilka said to her mother. "I'll come to New York for the holidays."

————

It takes time to fit a key into other people's doors, particularly when the phone inside is ringing, ringing, ringing. Alpha Stone wanted to welcome Ilka to Concordance. "We want to have you over as soon as the new semester settles in."

Personnel had found Ilka the little house of an assistant professor on sabbatical. Ilka picked up a scattering of letters behind the door: E. D. Rasmussen; Prof. E. Rasmussen, Ph.D., and a handwritten envelope for Mrs. E. Rasmussen from one E. Lipton in Madison, WI. The Rasmussens' living room was upholstered in tweed, a worn and grubby orange. Ilka deduced little children. The stillness in the air suggested recent agitation, palpable absences like the absence of newly dead people. Ilka carried bags up the stairs, opened a door and stood smelling the alien temperature of other people's bedrooms. She looked inside their closet. They were young people, strapped for money, collectors of checkered flannel bargain shirts in sharp, sad colors. Ilka felt their hurry, their wanting to fold themselves way back into the corners, with the children asking a lot of questions, children going berserk with intimations of a future in which they would not be anybody's only business. The bed was covered with something too green. It had the wrong kind of sheen. Ilka chose not to touch it.

Only one other upstairs room: One youth bed, a framed motto on the wall said "GOD LOVES JILL" in cross-stitch.

Back in the master bedroom Ilka took her shoes off, got her list of Concordance numbers and the Rasmussens' telephone, and lay down on the Rasmussens' green bed cover: it had a glassy surface, colder than human skin. At a point in time, without her being aware of having made a decision in the matter, Ilka was dialing the number of the woman who had dated the man whose name Ilka was never able to remember, so she was relieved when they didn't answer. She dialed the number Leina Shapiro had given her. They didn't answer. She dialed Jacquelyn Rosen's number and when they didn't answer, Ilka felt snubbed. Ilka lay on the Rasmussens' green cover. She lay and lay.

Tuesday Ilka redialed her first number and a woman's pleasant voice said, "I think she moved to New York. I'm sorry." She sounded sorry—a gently brought-up voice that had always had its questions answered when it was young. "I could give you the number of someone I think would know her number in New York."

"Thanks," Ilka said, "but I don't actually know her. A man I know in New York knew her in Ann Arbor and gave me her number. I've just moved to Concordance." Ilka meant, Why don't you invite me over for a cup of coffee, but said, "Thanks. Sorry."

Wednesday Ilka dialed the number Herbert had given her, and a child's voice, neither male nor female, said, "They're out. Whoa! Wait! This is them now. Hold it."

"Never mind," said Ilka and heard the child say, "Dad this is a woman on the phone."

In the unseen room the unseen telephone changed hands. The dad's voice said, "Who?"

Ilka said, "I'm new, at the institute. My friend Herbert Meadmore gave me your number and said I should give a call."

"Herbert *Who?*"

"You don't know Herbert Meadmore? I think . . ." Ilka flushed. The number Herbert had told her to call was the number underneath the number she had dialed. If this was the number Jules had given her she might be talking to the man whose brother-in-law played golf with the best friend of Winterneet's lawyer. Ilka said, "Do you know Jules McCartin?" but the man must have removed the receiver from his ear. Ilka heard him calling to someone out in a hallway or a foyer, or it might be a kitchen, "Do we know a Herbert? Charlie, please take the bag from your mother, she has her hands full, as you can plainly see. Joanne, do we know any Herbert? There's a woman on the phone." The man's voice came back full strength and said, "What did you say his name was?"

Ilka said, "Jules McCartin. It doesn't matter . . ."

"Hold on." The man shouted "HERBERT McCARTIN!" and the woman's tiny voice, distant and distinct, said, "*Into* the refrigerator, Charlie, please. You are quite as capable as anybody else in this family of opening a refrigerator door. Get the bag out of the trunk, please, Charlie, *close* the refrigerator door. Wasn't it Herbert Something, on the Hellenic cruise that we went with to— what's the restaurant called—on Samos or was that Skiathos? Ask her if he went on a Hellenic cruise."

The man shouted, "Why the hell don't you come and talk with her?" and the tiny voice shouted, "Because I'm the hell putting the goddamn ice cream in the goddamn freezer."

Ilka said, "It doesn't matter . . ." but the man in her ear said, "Did Herbert go on a Hellenic cruise—Joanne," he yelled, "was that four years ago?"

Ilka said, "Herbert has never been to Greece. I don't know about Jules McCartin."

Now the woman had taken the receiver. "Do you know Mary Anne Popper? She was on our cruise."

"No I don't," said Ilka. "What a lot of people there are that one doesn't know!"

"That's a fact," said the woman.

Institute people were expected to make a portion of time available to the university. Would Ilka like to teach English 206, Conversational English, Thursdays 6–7 in Philosophy Hall, Room 777?

Ilka said, "Good evening," put down her books, and made the mistake of catching the eye of the plump, freckled woman, front row, center seat, who was never after to let Ilka go. Ilka was aware of the pull of the orange-brown gaze as she addressed, lamely enough, the eight adult students: "We'll go around and introduce ourselves. Tell the class your name, please, and where you come from. I will begin. My name is Ilka. I was born in Vienna."

"I am coming also from Vienna but after I have lived always in Montevideo!" said the woman in the front row.

Ilka said, "'I *come* from Vienna. *After that* I always *lived in* . . .'"

The freckled woman asked, "Which *Bezirk* you are coming from?"

"'Which *district*,'" enunciated Ilka, "'do you *come* from?'"

"From Twenty-one," said the freckled woman.

Ilka said, "Please, tell the class your name."

"Gerti Gruner," said the woman.

Gathering her books at the end of class, Ilka avoided the hot and unremitting gaze from behind the students who had come to stand around the teacher's desk, but Gerti Gruner walked out the door and walked down the corridor to the elevators beside Ilka. She placed herself in front of Ilka and said, "When you have your hours in your office?"

"Oh," said Ilka, "I don't rate an office. I don't have hours." She leaned back to increase the distance between Gerti Gruner's eyes looking at too close a range into Ilka's eyes. Ilka closed and reopened her eyes and Gerti Gruner was looking into them. Ilka took a step backward and Gerti took a step forward to reestablish the original range and said, "You come to my house, isn't it? I cook Viennese."

Ilka said, "Well, thank you! Maybe some time when the semester has settled in."

Gerti Gruner came down the elevator and walked out of the building beside Ilka. Ilka stopped and said, "Well, good-bye."

"Which way you are going?" Gerti Gruner asked Ilka.

"Which way are you going?" Ilka asked Gerti Gruner.

"I am going that," said Gerti Gruner.

"Well," said Ilka. "I go this."

"I can go this also," said Gerti Gruner. She walked with a tight, short-stepping walk. Ilka felt her bobbing along. They passed the Bernstines' house, and the Bernstines were sitting on their covered porch with Alpha and Dr. Alfred Stone. They saw Ilka and waved. Ilka and Gerti passed the Ayes' house, and they were sitting on their lawn with the Zees.

On Friday Ilka called the number Leina had given her, which had not answered the first time, and they didn't answer. Ilka lay on top of the Rasmussens' slick green cover. After a while she dialed the number Jacquelyn had given her and was shocked when a woman's voice said, "Yes?"

Ilka said, "Could I speak to Norma?"

"This is Norma."

"Oh. Hi! Jacquelyn Rosen told me to give you a call."

"Oh? Yes? How is Jacquelyn?"

"Jacquelyn is fine. She told me to call you and say hello. I'm new in Concordance. And Jacquelyn told me to give you a call."

"Well, isn't that nice of you!" said Norma. "Give Jacquelyn my love when you see her."

"Jacquelyn is in New York," said Ilka. "I'm a new assistant at the institute."

"Well, if you write to Jacquelyn," said Norma, "give her my love."

"I sure will."

Saturday Ilka called Leina's number, which had not answered the first or the second time, and they did not answer. So much for them.

Sunday Maria Zee called. Winterneet should be back from the Coast Tuesday and they might be having people over. Would Ilka look on her calendar and see if she would be free Tuesday?

Ilka's calendar showed that she was free Tuesday. She was free Wednesday, Friday, Saturday, Sunday and Monday, but on Thursday Ilka waited by the elevators to go up to her class. All the elevators were going down to the basement cafeteria.

"That's Murphy!" said a black woman whose grand woolen skirt Ilka had been admiring. The woman wore a witty jacket with a lot of zippers. She met Ilka's smile with a lift of the left corner of her mouth.

Ilka said, "You know German?"

"I'm afraid not."

"German has a phrase: *Die Tücke des Objekts*. 'The spite of the inanimate object.'"

The woman laid her head back with a marvelous laugh. Both elevator doors opened and Ilka followed the interesting black woman into the left one and said, "My name is Ilka Weisz. I teach English for Foreigners but I'm really with the institute."

The woman said, "Sylvia Brandon. Sociology." Both women raised both corners of their lips.

Ilka looked up Sylvia Brandon in the directory and wrote her—Ilka thought it was a charming note—telling her that she was new in Concordance and asking her to have a cup of coffee in the cafeteria next Thursday.

Maria Zee called Friday. Winterneet had not returned from the Coast, but they were definitely wanting to have Ilka over and would give her a call.

There was no answering note from Sylvia Brandon. Ilka was surprised.

Ilka dialed Leina's number. Try just once more. A man said, "Marty Friedman."

Ilka said, "Leina told me to give you a call. I'm new in Concordance."

The man said, "We must have you over. Let me put Sally on."

Sally Friedman said, "It's just my brother is coming in from Toronto Wednesday. It's not that I don't love the little boys, they're darling, eight, six and two, but I just started a new job . . ."

"I know what that's like!" said Ilka. "I'm new at the institute."

"I'll give you a call," said Sally Friedman. "What did you say your name was?"

Thursday Gerti Gruner backed Ilka into the corner of the elevator and asked her when she was coming to Viennese supper in her house.

Ilka said, "You know how it is, starting a new job." Gerti Gruner bobbed along the street beside Ilka. The Bernstines' porch was dark. Ilka and Gerti passed the Ayes' house and they were sitting on their lawn with the Stones and the Bernstines. They did not see Ilka. Gerti Gruner said, "You like *Schlagobers*, yes?"

Joe Bernstine called Ilka to invite her to a reception for the Shakespeares on Sunday. He hoped Ilka was free.

Sylvia Brandon did not, and appeared not to be going to, answer Ilka's note. Ilka puzzled and puzzled about it: A stupid cup of coffee! Why would this woman even bother to not have it? Had Ilka's note been offensively charming?

The next Thursday Gerti Gruner looked Ilka in the eyes and asked her if she knew the Türkenschanz Park. Ilka backed a step away from her and said, "I don't remember much about Vienna. I left when I was seven." Gerti stepped a step closer and said, "In the Türkenschanz have I been every Sunday afternoon with my Opapa and Omama." They walked along the street. Gerti said, "Every Sunday there have always come to the Türkenschanz all the whole Vienna aunts, uncles, and my cousin Hedi and my cousins Albert and Roserl."

Ilka said, "I remember the *Kaffeehaus* corner Josephstädterstrasse. Every table had a glass with rolled wafers that looked like pencils."

"*Hohlhippen!*" said Gerti Gruner.

"Before we left, the waiter counted how many were left and my father paid for the ones I'd eaten."

Gerti said, "Every time when they have brought a cup of coffee, they have brought also a glass water and afterwards counted the glasses. All the aunts and uncles always knew that we were all the whole Sunday afternoon at the Türkenschanz and they have come with the cousins and have sat and have drunk coffee. In the evening have we ordered always *Schnitzerl*."

Ilka said, "*Sacher Torte* and my father read the newspapers on bamboo sticks they kept on a rack on a marble column. Here's where you came in"—Ilka drew the geography of the Café Josephstadt corner of Josephstädterstrasse in the Eighth District in Vienna, on the air of Concordance, Connecticut. "Here was the window. Here was the door where the waiters went in and out, here was the marble column with the rack of newspapers, and here is where we always sat."

Gerti said, "You come to my house. I make *Wiener Schnitzerl*. I make *Sacher Torte* with *Schlagobers*."

Sunday Joe Bernstine walked Ilka and Martin Moses, a tall young man whom Ilka had seen around the institute, out onto the covered porch to meet Leslie Shakespeare. The new director had a fine head, and eyes so blue Ilka could look through them to the sky behind his back. Having nothing particular to say to the two young people before him, the new director said nothing, looked at each of them with interest, and shook their hands. They passed back into the living room to allow other people to come out and be introduced.

Ilka and Martin Moses stood where they could watch the new director out on the porch, talking to a circle of people, surrounded by the circle of people waiting to talk to him. Martin Moses said, "I should have said something to him. I couldn't think of anything to say!"

Ilka said, "You know those Egyptian sculptures that have one figure a different order of magnitude from all the other figures? They're perfectly realistic! Leslie Shakespeare is larger than anyone at this party, and I bet he was only another skinny schoolboy. Joe Bernstine is quite a small person but he outweighs . . ."

"Me," said six-foot Martin Moses.

"The senior wives take up more room," Ilka said. Ilka and Martin Moses watched Mrs. Shakespeare talking with a group of junior people who from time to time laughed. Ilka had had nobody to listen to her theories since New York and she said, "I bet you Socrates is always the largest person at a party, but so are Rockefeller, Helen of Troy, and the King of England. Which one is Winterneet?"

"Wouldn't know him if he bit me," said Martin Moses.

"As soon as we know which one he is, he'll be the largest person at this party. Which is Winterneet?" Ilka asked Joe Bernstine, who was passing.

Joe said, "He couldn't make it. Very bad cold. I was on the phone with him this morning. He was upset. He's fond of Leslie."

"How did they meet?" asked Ilka, but Joe had moved on to rescue a guest who was standing by herself: Sylvia Brandon in her grand skirt. She wore a beautiful silver sweater. Ilka wanted it.

Martin Moses was saying, "Never been to a party yet where Winterneet has actually showed up. If you're free Friday come to a shindig I'm throwing for a lot of graduate student types. Winterneet is guaranteed not to show. Winterneet is not invited. I'm going out and say something to Leslie Shakespeare." Martin Moses walked out onto the porch, and Ilka went over to Sylvia Brandon and said, "I'm Ilka Weisz."

Sylvia Brandon said, "I'm Sylvia Brandon."

Ilka said, "We met at the elevators when they were all going to the basement."

Sylvia Brandon said, "I'll get our statisticians to do a study of the laws of improbability."

Now Jenny Bernstine cried, "Someone be brave! It would be a public service to start the salmon. Sylvia! Ilka! Somebody!"

People were moving in from the porch. Ilka saw the new director momentarily alone, slipped out, and said, "I have a theory," and told him about the Egyptian sculpture. It seemed to take a very long time.

The new director said, "I understand that we've got you teaching in the adult program at the university."

"English for Foreigners. I'm a foreigner," said Ilka in despair: once embarked on this routine of self-conscious inanities there's no way back to good sense and propriety. If Ilka had met herself at this moment, at this party, she would have written herself off as an ass and walked away. The new director with the beautiful head and the English voice did not walk away and seemed not to be looking for some better opportunity over Ilka's shoulder. He regarded her attentively, without pretending to any peculiar interest. Ilka understood that she was talking to a patient man who might choose to distinguish between an ass and a person showing off at a party. Ilka said, "Talking to you makes people nervous. I wonder if my students feel like that talking to me?"

Leslie Shakespeare's eyes widened ever so slightly; he could be seen to be thinking. He said, "Probably so." Ilka was relieved and sorry when Joe Bernstine came to fetch his guest of honor. "Leslie, we need you to circulate. We need you to come in and eat."

The new director said, "Well then, that's what I'll do." He looked behind him, saw nobody, and putting his hand not on but just in back of Ilka's back, moved her through the door ahead of him: he was not going to leave anybody alone on the empty porch.

"It is possible," Ilka said to Martin Moses at the buffet table, "that our new director is a nice man."

The day after the reception Alpha Stone called to invite Ilka for drinks. Sally Friedman called. Her brother and the little boys had gone back to Toronto. Was Ilka free for dinner? Alicia Aye invited Ilka for cocktails, and Thursday Gerti looked Ilka in the eyes and asked her if her blouse was from Vienna? Ilka said, "I was seven when I left Vienna." Gerti Gruner said, "This pattern is reminding of the blouse of my Tante dead in Belsen," so then Ilka asked Gerti if she would like to have a cup of coffee in the cafeteria. But where had Gerti Gruner gone?

Ilka saw Gerti's back diminishing down the perspective of the corridor in pursuit of a man who stopped and turned out to be Professor Zee. Professor Zee's right leg and right shoulder remained set in the direction in which he had been, and would have liked to continue, going. He was leaning a little backward from what Gerti was saying to him at too close a range. Whatever she was saying had a certain length and several parts. Ilka watched Gerti's head and plump shoulders working with that slight agitation which accompanies the act of speaking. The elevator came, opened, and closed. Professor Zee's mouth opened. What he said was brief. Gerti's shoulders went back into action and when they ceased, Professor Zee walked on. Gerti Gruner turned, increasing in size up the corridor toward Ilka. "I ask Professor Zee when he has his hour in his office."

The cafeteria was a depressed area. There was a coffee automat and a sandwich automat. Ilka revolved the display of sad buns with their evil fillings and said, "Hope must certainly spring eternal. Every time I come down I'm looking for something wonderful to have materialized." But where had Gerti gone? Ilka saw her backing Professor Sylvia Brandon into the opposite wall. Gerti Gruner's shoulders went into converse with Professor Brandon, who was looking directly at Ilka. Ilka could tell that Sylvia Brandon did not recognize her.

"Winterneet is not invited. Pizza is in the kitchen," Martin Moses said as he welcomed each guest at the door. The rooms were small. There were too many people in the kitchen. Ilka's triangle of pizza behaved like Dali's watch and kept folding away from her mouth. Ilka carried her glass of wine into the other room. Martin Moses was sitting on a mattress on the floor with an attractive lot of younger people leaning their backs against the wall. He budged everybody over to make room for Ilka. He had a gallon bottle of white wine on his lap and topped off Ilka's glass. The young people were high and tended to hilarity. The mattress was covered with a lightweight cotton throw that had an Indian pattern and tended to bunch. Ilka kept wanting to smooth it back over the exposed black-and-white ticking. The mattress was inching away from the wall. Everybody got up to push it back, and that's when Ilka saw Gerti Gruner standing in the doorway. Gerti was staring at Ilka. Ilka asked Martin Moses to change places with her and sat down with her back to Gerti.

Martin Moses asked, "Why is Gerti Gruner staring daggers at you?"

"Because she keeps inviting me to supper and I'm never available and here I am in your house, at your party. That's horrible, isn't it—talking about her right behind her back?"

"Behind your back, actually," said Martin Moses.

Ilka said, "I have a theory that Gerti Gruner used to be a plump, pretty Viennese girl with one of those delicious chins, so she thinks when she wants something she is going to get it, and what she wants is me."

"Aha?" said Martin Moses with interest.

"No, I mean to be her Viennese cousin and Vienna is so long ago. It's sad, actually," Ilka said, "because I'm in possession of a piece of information not available to Gerti Gruner: Gerti Gruner can't have me. Is she still standing in the door?"

"Still staring daggers," reported Martin Moses.

"There's a Viennese expression: '*Nicht mit der Hacken ʒu der-schlagen.*' It means something like 'With an axe you couldn't do her in.' I have several theories about Gerti Gruner," Ilka said, all the time wishing she were not saying these things to Martin Moses, whom she hardly knew. Ilka kept hoping—she kept meaning—to stop, nevertheless she kept right on, and Martin Moses kept filling up her glass from his bottle. "One theory," said Ilka, "is Gerti Gruner is missing the human component that tells one person that she is being a pest to another person, or, two, Gerti Gruner knows she is being a pest and doesn't mind it. I actually think there's something ever so slightly the matter with Gerti Gruner. She looks one right in the eyes which is not a thing normal people do to each other."

"Sure they do," said Martin Moses.

"Look into my eyes," said Ilka. "*Into*, not *at* my eyes." Martin looked into Ilka's eyes, blinked and looked away. Ilka said, "We think we look into each other's eyes because the language says we do, but the language is wrong."

"People we love we look in the eyes," Martin said.

"We do not. Particularly people we make love with, particularly when we are making love with them. That's when we *close* our eyes. I think I better go home."

But in the front door stood Gerti Gruner barring Ilka's exit. "Oh! Hello! So! How are you?" squealed Ilka.

"You come tomorrow to supper in my house," said Gerti Gruner, "isn't it?"

"I think I can't. Not tomorrow," said Ilka looking in her handbag for her date book. Ilka's date book confirmed that tomorrow Ilka was having dinner with the Stones.

"Sunday," said Gerti.

Sunday Ilka was having dinner with the Zees. Ilka's date book showed next week to be entirely filled up, which astonished Ilka, who continued to feel that her days were empty: These several events did not essentially count, because if the institute hadn't happened to have hired a new director, the Bernstines would not have given him a reception, and Alpha Stone would not have seen Ilka at it and remembered that they had been meaning to have her over, nor could she have introduced Ilka to Alicia Aye. These invitations didn't *prove* anything. If Ilka hadn't happened to have got talking with Martin Moses, she wouldn't have so much as *known* he was having a shindig. And, if she hadn't tried the Friedmans a fourth time, they wouldn't have so much as known of Ilka's existence, and then there would have been nobody all week except Gerti Gruner on Thursday. Ilka looked up and Gerti Gruner was looking daggers not, as a matter of fact, into Ilka's eyes: Gerti Gruner's eyes met not Ilka's eyes, but each other where their line of vision crossed at a point in front of the bridge of Ilka's nose.

"I make *Sacher Torte* with *Schlagobers*," said Gerti Gruner, who knew, as everybody always knows, and minded, as everybody minds, that she was being a pest. It was something she had learned to live with. What Gerti Gruner could not learn was how to survive in an absence of cousins.

THE TALK IN ELIZA'S KITCHEN

Alpha Stone said, "Winterneet couldn't make it. He's in Copenhagen."

"Never you mind Winterneet," said Ilka and looked gladly around the room full of her new friends and colleagues at the Concordance Institute. Here were her hosts Alpha and Alfred Stone, here were the Ayes and the Zees and the Cohns and the Bernstines. How could Ilka's back tell the difference between empty air and a body—male? Director Leslie Shakespeare was standing right behind Ilka listening to his wife Eliza making Yvette Gordot laugh. "Your wife is terrific," Ilka said to him.

"Yes, she is," said Director Shakespeare, and he and Ilka stood and listened together.

"That was before I stopped Leslie from doing the things he likes to do," Eliza Shakespeare was saying. She was Canadian, a plain woman nobly built on the grand scale, wide in the shoulders, with a length of thigh. Her hair was so fine and electrically charged it attached itself to her cheeks and temples. She had to keep palming it away.

Alpha called everyone into the dining room.

Ilka was seated between Professor Zee and Leslie Shakespeare and at the furthest remove from Mrs. Shakespeare who was entertaining her end of the table with a highly colored anecdote about a groom who had inadvertently locked Leslie into the stables, making him miss the equestrian tryouts for the Olympics. Ilka glanced at Leslie's great head brooding over his soup. "Did he really lock you in?" she asked him.

"No," said Leslie.

"Are you really an equestrian?"

"I was," said Leslie.

"No, you weren't," said Ilka, "and I can prove it."

Leslie looked at Ilka.

Ilka said, "People I sit next to at dinner are not equestrians, and I'm sitting next to you."

Leslie smiled.

"I can prove you never tried out for the Olympics."

Leslie laughed.

"People I know are as likely to try out for the Olympics as they are to climb Mount Everest."

Leslie blushed.

"You climbed Mount Everest!" Ilka said so loudly that Eliza said,

"Before I stopped him."

"Did Eliza stop you?" asked Ilka.

"As a matter of fact she did."

At the far end of the table Eliza was embarked on a tale about the sherpa who carried Leslie's tent out onto the blinding white expanse and disappeared. "Nothing as far as the eye could see except his abominable snow prints."

It felt silly to keep asking Leslie what, in Eliza's stories, was the truth. Ilka kept looking sideways at him. He said, "It was a preliminary expedition to test new equipment."

"And Leslie tested a new type of nylon rope by falling off a mountain and hanging upside down with a simultaneously spinning and yo-yoing motion . . ."

Here Leslie said, "Dear, did you ask Alpha for Mrs. Beaton's recipe for gooseberry fool? Our real estate man," persevered Leslie, "showed us two gooseberry bushes in our back garden. Did you know that growing gooseberries is forbidden in several states of the Union?" And having got the left side of the table discussing Mrs. Beaton's Cookery and the right side listing the obsolescent laws that continue on the books, Leslie returned to the soup in his plate. Ilka looked down the table at Eliza who had been stopped in the middle of her story. Eliza's head was bent over her plate and her eyes were hidden.

This was before Ilka got a car, and the Shakespeares offered to drive her home. She walked down the dark path with Eliza behind Professor Stone walking the director to his car. Eliza said, "It wasn't the gooseberries out back, it was the tiny tomatoes in the front that made Leslie buy the house."

Ilka sat beside Leslie. Eliza, in the backseat, said, "Alfred Stone looks like something out of *Steve Canyon*. The iron jaw, the jutting forelock."

"Tremendously good-looking," said Ilka.

"I don't think so!" said Leslie. "You think he is good-looking?"

"Yes," said Ilka and Eliza.

Ilka said, "By the way, do we know there really is a Winterneet?"

"There used to be, before he got his Nobel Prize," Eliza said.

"But you affirm, categorically, that Winterneet exists?" asked Ilka. "I cried when I had to leave New York and come to live in Concordance. All my friends said, 'Winterneet lives in Concordance.' My friend Jules knows someone who knows someone who played golf with someone who knows Winterneet. At my interview, Zack Zee told me Winterneet had done the institute a lecture series, and Jenny drove me by his house. Alpha said Winterneet was in Copenhagen. Maria promised to have him to dinner but he had not got back from the Coast. The Bernstines made you a reception, and he had a cold. Martin Moses invited me to a party given for the express purpose of not being stood up by Winterneet by the simple expedient of not inviting him."

Leslie said, "The State Department sends him on tours."

"We knew Winterneet before he was Winterneet," said Eliza. "Winnie was our 'lodger' and the day the baby disappeared he skedaddled. Got out of town."

Ilka would have very much liked to hear more but was obliged to say, "That's my house at the corner. I rent it from the Rasmussens. They're on sabbatical."

"Leslie, aren't you going to be a gentleman and walk Ilka up the path to her front door?"

"Ilka, do you need to be walked to your front door?"

"Absolutely not," said Ilka stoutly, and Leslie invited her to come Sunday morning.

Eliza said, "To a late breakfast."

Ilka walked up her path in a state of happiness she had not experienced since New York: she liked the Shakespeares so much, and they had invited her to a late breakfast.

Leslie called Sunday morning. "I have chores in town. Eliza thought you might like me to pick you up on the way home."

Ilka was pleased. She kept inventing more hardships from which being picked up by Leslie was going to save her well past the point at which she perfectly understood his desire to get off the telephone.

"Is eleven a good time?"

Eleven was the perfect time by which Ilka would have finished grading her class papers. "This really is good of you . . ."

"Oh you bet," said Leslie.

Ilka experienced the intense pleasantness of sitting beside Leslie Shakespeare, but it made her nervous. She obligated herself to entertain Leslie's silence with speech, which, she hoped, was interesting without being tiresomely interesting. "Do you know that delicious moment when you have finished grading your last student and you have a whole week before you have to grade your next class?"

Leslie appeared to be thinking this over.

Ilka said, "It's like the second before a holiday has had the first minute bitten out of it?"

Now Leslie had two things to think over.

Ilka said, "Like the moment in the theater when the curtain has just started going up?"

Leslie said, "I know that moment."

Let him think up the next thing to say, but Leslie was turning in to his driveway. He walked Ilka into the kitchen to say hello to Eliza. "Can I help?" Ilka asked her.

"Christ, no!" said Eliza. "Leslie will make us Bloody Marys."

Leslie and Ilka took their drinks into the living room. Ilka said, "I don't know how you do it, but you and Eliza make me talk. You never ask me any questions, and I tell you everything I know."

"That *is* odd," said Leslie. When Ilka's glass was empty he carried it out into the kitchen, and she heard him say, "Ilka says we never ask her questions and she tells us everything. She says, how do we do that?" Ilka imagined Eliza standing with her back to Leslie because she could not hear the answer. Ilka got up and stood in the doorway and listened, and hearing Leslie's returning footsteps, sat quickly down.

Leslie said, "Eliza says we ask questions in the form of suppositions."

Ilka said, "The truth of the matter is that you and Eliza are accomplished listeners. I'm always interjecting my autobiography into the other person's story. I mean to be expressing my sympathetic understanding, but all it does is take the conversation away from the other speaker. What you do is make little sounds like *mm* or *mf*, so that one feels you listening. Do you know what you do when somebody says something you don't like?"

"What?" asked Leslie.

"You uncross your right leg from over your left knee and recross your left leg over your right knee."

"I'll be damned," said Leslie.

"If I see you make some abrupt movement like suddenly picking up or putting down your glass, I know I've got some common fact dead wrong."

Leslie said again that he would be damned, excused himself and walked out into the kitchen to tell Eliza what Ilka had said. He came back and said, "Eliza says we should bring our drinks and talk in the kitchen."

Eliza once more refused Ilka's offer of help. Ilka and Leslie sat at the table while Eliza sliced and chopped and grated. It was a large and pleasant kitchen. Two snapshots, one of a little baby with a large bib, and one of an apple tree in full fruit, were stuck into the frame of the window.

Ilka said, "The Rasmussens' kitchen is full of doodads. When I moved in, I hid things away in back of the cupboard and went shopping. I bought this beautiful Danish chopping board made of blocks of different kinds of wood."

"Did you? I fished this one," Eliza pointed to a little square of wood with a cracked corner, "out of Lake Michigan in 1959."

Leslie said, "Tell Eliza what you said about the way I listen."

Ilka repeated to Eliza what she had said, and Eliza asked, "How do I listen?"

"You look pleased when you hear some half-truth or nonsense; you get a satisfied look, as if the world were bearing out the opinion you privately held of it." Ilka was excited to feel them listening to what she was saying; she hoped she would be able to stop talking. She said, "In the weeks I've known you I've told you all my stories, but I know very little about you," and she asked what Eliza meant about asking questions in the form of suppositions.

Eliza said, "If you ask me point-blank how I lost my baby"— here Leslie got out of his chair and walked to the sink and stood beside Eliza, "—I'd say what my rotten little American cousins used to say to me—like 'Mind your own beeswax,' or, 'That's for me to know and you to find out.' But suppose you said, 'It must have been a warm day when you left the baby in her stroller in front of the door?' I might say, 'Actually, it was one of those lovely-looking April days'"—Eliza walked to the refrigerator and Leslie kept beside her—"'that *looked* warm, or maybe I was longing for the Chicago winter to be over. When we got outside it was chilly.'" Leslie walked to the stove with Eliza. "I put the brakes on the stroller, ran in, got her blanket that I had already washed and put away, and out fell a box of mothballs, so I ran and got the broom and dustpan and I'll drive Leslie crazy telling you the whole story."

"Just what my mother does," said Ilka. "She tells the whole story of how she left my father sitting on the side of the road before Obernpest a week before the end of the war, and she never saw him again."

Drivers in American movies made poor Ilka nervous, the way they took their eyes off the road to make love to the person in the seat beside them. Leslie kept his blue eye fully forward, leaving

Ilka at liberty to study his fine head, the stern upper lip, the cheek with its high, healthy male fairness. "I did it again!" she said. "I told my father-story and stopped Eliza talking about the baby!"

"She will tell it to you again," Leslie said.

"How long ago was this?"

"It will be fifteen years next April 15."

"Doesn't the pain pale?"

Leslie thought about this and said, "It seemed intolerable when it happened, and it seems intolerable today."

Ilka resented the Shakespeares' intolerable loss. She imagined it like a wound in their lives, a flaw in their pleasures that flawed the pleasure she wanted to be at liberty to feel when she was with them. Ilka wished the baby unlost.

Before he left her off at her gate, Leslie invited Ilka to breakfast the following Sunday. Again he called and offered to pick her up. Again Ilka worried about not helping, but what Eliza wanted was for Ilka and Leslie to sit and drink their Bloody Marys in the kitchen and talk where she could hear them. She said, "Winnie's back. He wanted to come for breakfast, but I said we had other plans."

"I'll phone him later," said Leslie.

"I told him to come get his boxes."

"What's Winterneet like?" asked Ilka.

"A Peanuts cartoon," replied Eliza. "A swelled head walking on his little shoes."

"You don't like him?" Ilka asked doubtfully.

Leslie said, "Winterneet and the Bernstines are our oldest American friends."

"How did you meet him?" asked Ilka.

Leslie said, "When we were graduate students in Chicago, Winnie was an adjunct professor. Everybody was short of money.

Winnie's marriage with Dorothy was breaking up and he moved in with us—"

"—and having spread his papers over every surface of every room in the apartment," Eliza said, "he moved out . . ."

Leslie uncrossed and recrossed his legs.

". . . and moved in with Susanna," Eliza said. "Leslie collected the papers into a cardboard box that I fell over in our foyer all summer and autumn. Come the first snow I put it out in the driveway."

"You didn't!" said Ilka.

"Yes, I did," said Eliza.

Ilka looked at Leslie, who said, "She did."

"Leslie brought it in and carried it to his study. When Winnie left Susanna he moved back with his second box of papers."

"You know what I love?" Ilka said when Leslie presently stood up, handling his car keys inside his jacket pocket. "I like it that you let a person know when you've had enough of them."

"Always the gentleman," said Eliza.

"No, but it means I can sit and enjoy myself without worrying whether the time has come for me to offer to go home. Eliza and Leslie, I make you a proposition: Will you be my elective cousins? I'm low on the kind one has by blood."

Leslie and Eliza agreed to be Ilka's elective cousins, and Eliza invited her to come over after dinner, Saturday. The Bernstines were dropping by for drinks. Leslie said he would pick her up.

Saturday, and Ilka walked into the Shakespeares' living room. On a chair, with a drink in his hand, sat a man whose graying orange hair was the color, exactly, of the expanse of his cranium. He had a flat face with shallow features—the nose was blunt and short, the eye-sockets lacked shadow. His shoes were child-sized. It was the actual Winterneet regarding Ilka with a smile that revealed a small, charming gap between the two upper front teeth. Ilka lowered her eyes, raised them, and the actual Winterneet was still smiling at her. Here came the Bernstines. Leslie brought drinks and Eliza a platter of what Winterneet, with his delightful smile, called the "eats."

Ilka meant to keep looking intelligently engaged in a conversation these old friends must have been having together for the past decades. Once in a while Leslie threw Ilka a scrap of data, a gloss on a name: "It was Frank who introduced Susanna and Winterneet in sixty-three, wasn't it? Susanna was Dave Foster's half sister," Leslie explained.

"Aha!" Ilka kept saying.

The phone rang. Leslie walked out into the hall.

"Sixty-four is when we had the baby . . ." said Eliza—Ilka observed Joe Bernstine plant his hands on the arms of his chair, ready to rise, saw Jenny's forehead corrugate—"and you removed yourself to Berkeley. In sixty-five," Eliza said to Winterneet, "your three boxes moved to Amherst with us." Joe settled back; Jenny's face continued anxious.

Winterneet said, "When I get back from London, I'll come over and spend the day, and sort out what I want to throw away."

Leslie returned, "It's Una. She's at Kennedy."

Eliza said, "Tell her no."

Leslie said, "She just got in from London."

Eliza said, "No."

Leslie went out.

Winnie asked, "And how is our little Una?"

"I was happy, until a minute ago, to have heard nothing about little Una for the last six months," said Eliza.

"She wrote me," said Leslie returning into the room.

"Well, I was happy to hear nothing about it," said Eliza.

"Well, I thought you would be happy," said Leslie.

"Little Una in the granny dress with straw in her hair!" said Winterneet.

"That," said Eliza, "is our Una."

The Bernstines offered to give Ilka a lift home. Winterneet said he'd stay if someone would offer him a nightcap.

In the car Ilka asked the Bernstines about Una.

"Poor Una! Fell rather in love with Leslie and Eliza. Leslie-and-Eliza."

"I can understand that," said Ilka.

"The Shakespeares brought her back to the States with them. Her father is the theologian, Paul Thayer."

"Uncle" said Joe, and they argued about Una's relationship to this Paul Thayer until they arrived at Ilka's gate.

Sunday morning Leslie called and fetched Ilka in the car. Ilka walked into Eliza's kitchen and there was Winterneet sitting at the table smiling at Ilka.

Ilka was not some young thing; it annoyed her not to be able to keep up her end—like Eliza, who could cut and slice, correct the seasoning, and perform last-minute maneuvers at the stove and keep the conversation flying like some high-wire act. Ilka developed a crick in the neck looking from a joke of Eliza's to Winterneet, who swung with it into a mutual reminiscence. Eliza, tossing and tasting the salad, elaborated a very tall tale that Winterneet topped with a deliciously nasty quip. Ilka wanted to play with them, up there, in the middle air, but the palpitation of her heart preempted her breathing. Ilka hunkered down waiting for the laughter to run its course before she took the running start to get her own joke airborne with enough breath for the punch line, but Eliza, removing her beautiful French bread from the oven, had started a story that grew naturally out of Winterneet's point, which Ilka missed, because it took off from what she suspected herself of not having recognized as a quotation. Ilka crouched to wait for the next opening in the hope of having thought of something that would fit whatever might by that time be under discussion.

Leslie, leaning back in his chair, observed his wife and his friend with the air of a man eating the best bread and butter, and listening to the best conversation, in his own house, at his own breakfast. Eliza had glided two coddled eggs onto Leslie's plate when the doorbell rang. Leslie looked regretful, got reluctantly up, and went to answer the door. He came back. He said, "Dear. It's Una."

"Tell her no," Eliza said.

"She's come straight from the airport," said Leslie. "She has her bags."

Eliza said, "I recommend the Concordance Hotel, corner Euclid and Main, a clean, well-lighted place."

Leslie went out.

"You can't do that! Can you do that?" asked Ilka in an excited whisper. "Can you tell someone to go away?"

"Watch me," said Eliza. "Or watch me tell Leslie to tell her."

"But I mean—imagine having just arrived from New York . . ."

"From London," Eliza corrected her.

"What can you say to her?"

"You say, 'If you bother me, I'll set the Concordance police on you.'"

Leslie returned. Eliza gave him back the eggs she had kept warm for him and said, "I make Leslie go and do the dirty work."

"Yes, you do," said Leslie.

Ilka said, "What were the actual words you said to her?"

"I said, 'There's a nice enough family hotel on Main—medium priced.' I wrote the address on a piece of paper and hugged her good-bye."

"You hugged Una!" cried Eliza.

"Yes," said Leslie.

"She's Paul Thayer's niece, no?" asked Winterneet.

"Niece by marriage," Leslie said. The doorbell rang again. Eliza took Leslie's eggs and covered them with foil.

When Leslie came back he had his jacket on and the car-keys in his fist. "Her driver has driven off. I'll take her to the hotel."

"She's driven her driver off!" said Eliza. "Our little Una likes Leslie to drive her. Una is always having to be driven. Una always needs picking up."

Ilka said, "You must have once liked her?"

"Una is a chilly English schoolgirl who came to America and caught the Sixties."

"Why isn't that a good thing for a chilly English girl to catch?"

"Because she had to work so hard at it. Have you ever seen a hedonist with gritted teeth?"

"Poor Una," said Ilka.

"Poor, poor Una," said Eliza. "Like the baby kangaroo in Pooh Corner who keeps jumping out of its mother's pouch, saying 'Look at me jumping!' Una jumped into everybody's bed saying, 'Look at me screwing!'"

"But you have to imagine having been born chilly. What was Una *supposed* to do?" Ilka looked to Winterneet for acquiescence. Winterneet was eating Leslie's coddled eggs. Ilka said, "Don't you think there's something gallant about warming yourself up by your own bootstraps? What do you want her to *do*?"

"Go back to London," said Eliza.

When Leslie returned from driving Una to the Concordance Hotel, he drove Ilka home to the Rasmussens'.

Eliza was not present at the institute reception which poor Una gate-crashed.

Ensconced together in the embrasure of the window, Leslie and Una looked like the classic couple one pretends not to notice on a couch, or a park bench—she in tears, he consoling, implicated and sorry, but one knows the trouble is all her own. You imagine one story and another story and all the stories you imagine will hit the nail beside the head. Leslie offered Una his hand-kerchief and watched her blow her nose. Seeing Ilka looking in their direction, he beckoned. He introduced them.

Una stared at the new entity before her with humorless eyes. She was a lovely, clever-looking young woman. Her no-bra, bedroom-hair style seemed grafted onto a Reynolds beauty. Una's little, elegant face was exaggeratedly shapely and pointed, her mouth tiny, moist. Instead of an amplitude of crackling satin, Una wore an anorexic pair of jeans. She sobbed. She said, "Isn't the criminal supposed to be told her crime? What did I do that was so wrong? Why has Eliza dropped me? I rang her on the telephone, and she picked up and said that she was out."

Ilka and Leslie did not smile. Una had begun to cry again. Leslie offered to drive her back to the hotel. "You want a ride?" he asked Ilka, who understood that she was wanted as a buffer.

Ilka, in the backseat, was no help in stemming Una's grief at her expulsion from Eliza's kitchen. "All I want is to sit down face-to-face and talk this thing out!"

"Talking out face-to-face is an overrated activity," said Leslie sadly. At the hotel he got out and walked the weeping young woman to the door, hugged her good-bye, and patted his pocket, but Una had pocketed his handkerchief.

Leslie got back into the car and said, "Come to the house?"

"Love to."

Here was Winterneet, sitting at the kitchen table. Eliza was on a tear. "I can't pick up the telephone without finding Una crying on the other end. Leslie, remember the day Una wove a circle around you thrice?"

"Around us both, you and me," said Leslie.

"Doesn't a Jewish bride walk circles around her groom?" Eliza asked Ilka.

"Does she? I'm not a very efficient Jew."

"She's a spider spinning you into her web," said Eliza.

"The magic circle," said Leslie.

"A mandala," said Winterneet. "Una was incorporating you. Our Una was into a little bit of witchcraft?"

"'Into' witchcraft, as you are 'into' destroying the language," said Eliza, but Winterneet said he was rather fond of this "being into" things and grinned into Ilka's eyes. It was a nice example of what Mencken called "judicious neology," he said, but offered to give it up if Eliza could come up with another English formulation that expressed that particular human relation to a human activity.

"It's a syntactic barbarism," said Eliza. They were off. Leslie leaned back and smiled at them. Ilka was jealous.

Ilka did not think that she had impressed herself on Una's consciousness so she was surprised, when she answered the Rasmussens' front-door bell, to find the girl on her doorstep. "Leslie gave me your address," said Una. Una had come to talk about the Shakespeares. "It's like living a who-done-it that starts with the hanging, and it's me being hanged. I mean, what did I do? I think it was the ice cream," said Una. "Eliza once made ice cream and it tasted lovely, and I *told* her it tasted lovely, but I shouldn't have said I liked the consistency of the bought kind, because she didn't talk to me the rest of the meal."

"We are so weird," said Ilka, "the way we can none of us bear being faulted."

"But I wasn't even faulting her. I didn't say I didn't like her ice cream; all I said was I liked the consistency of the bought kind."

"Say I'm wearing a blue dress," said Ilka, "and you say, 'Green is a nice color,' and I think, 'I'm never going to talk to Una ever again.'"

"That's ridiculous!"

"That's what I mean," said Ilka. "We are, all of us, ridiculous. All we can hear is somebody saying we are less than perfect. And it's not as if we hadn't already got that figured out for ourselves."

"I never mind being told when I'm wrong."

Ilka said, "Will you forgive me if I don't believe you?"

"What I can't stand," said Una, "is not being told what I'm supposed to have done! I don't understand people not sitting down face-to-face." Una wiped her eyes and said, "What I actually think is, I think my opinions are too difficult for Eliza to assimilate. She's Canadian, you know, very uptight. I threaten her because I hang loose." Ilka looked surreptitiously at her watch, but Una was just getting started.

Leslie beeped his horn outside Ilka's gate Sunday. "Eliza is on a rampage." A new phase had begun in what Eliza called the Una Wars. Leslie had gone to bed early as usual. Eliza, staying downstairs with her book, had raised her eyes and seen Una looking in the window.

The version Eliza told Ilka and Winterneet at the kitchen table was more elaborate. "I walk into the kitchen to get myself a glass of wine, walk back into the living room, settle myself on the sofa. Where's my book? Nothing like being in the middle of a book, and you don't know where you put it down. I get up, I walk around, I'm looking all around and there's this maenad—a bacchante—wild-eyed, hair full of fruit and leaves, looking in the window mouthing at me! I let out such a holler Leslie comes bounding downstairs—and it is something to see Leslie bounding in his striped blue pajamas."

Leslie said, "Eliza was going to call the police and report a trespasser."

"It was our Una peering through the cherry tomatoes! Leslie pulled on his trousers and drove her back to her hotel."

"My bell at the Rasmussens rang," said Ilka, "and it was Una come to complain about you."

"Can't open a door, or look through a window without finding Una on the other side."

The doorbell rang and Eliza said, "I'm calling the police." It was the town deli with a delivery: Una's peace offering, a heroic basket—a cornucopia. "Bourbon-spiked marmalade! That's disgusting," said Eliza.

"Let's try some," said Leslie.

"Canned jugged hare! Toss it out. Look at the size of the pears! They're obscene," said Eliza.

"The superfruit, in—what kind of still-life paintings am I thinking of?" said Leslie.

"The kind that has a worm crawling out of the apple, or a bug, a wasp. A spider."

Ilka said, "Eliza, you have to imagine being Una and not knowing what to do about you. I think she really is in pain."

"She's a pain in the neck," said Eliza.

"Really, though," Ilka said to Leslie when he drove her home, "what did Una do that made Eliza drop her?"

"Eliza and I," said Leslie, "dropped Una."

Ilka accepted the reprimand. In a moment she said, "Imagine you have friends you love, whose kitchen you are used to walking in and out of, and one day they will not let you in and won't tell you why."

Leslie was silent for such a long time that Ilka said, "Why won't you tell Una why?"

"I'm trying to think of the answer to your question," said Leslie. "I don't want to answer you until I have thought."

"Sorry."

"I'll get you a copy of Winterneet's little book called *Tales from the Mouth of God*. They're quite nice. In each of Winnie's tales, God rather irritably corrects a Bible story that misrepresents what he had in mind. God says, 'Why would I have expelled Adam and Eve for eating a fruit?' The trouble was they bored him, but he didn't want to tell them. It's devastating to know you are a bore, because it's not something you can do anything about. Kinder to let them think it was something they had done wrong, so they could live in the hope of stopping doing it and getting back into paradise. So God said, 'Let there be sin.'"

"Do you think Una is a bore?"

"Don't you think?"

Ilka said, "But wasn't she the same bore when you liked her and brought her to the States with you?"

"In another of Winnie's stories, God explains why he created falling in love, which makes the other person's sin smell like your own sin—that's to say, not at all. Ah, but the stink after we fall out of love, out of friendship!"

"That is so terrible!"

"Yes, it is," said Leslie.

Back in the kitchen Eliza was filling Winterneet's glass. She filled her own glass and said, "The phone rings. Una is strapped for money and the bank is about to close. Leslie runs over to drive her to the bank. The phone rings. Una is suicidal. Leslie runs over to catch her jumping out the window. 'You have to imagine being poor Una being strapped!'" said Eliza in a mincing voice, with an innocent gape of the eyes, and a Viennese roll of the "r", "'You have to imagine being suicidal!' I don't have to bloody imagine being suicidal! And I don't have to 'imagine' Una when I've got her bloody underfoot."

Winterneet tilted the empty salad bowl and picked out the pieces of arugala sticking to the sides.

———

Eliza was still going strong the following evening, at a dinner party at the Ayes. A letter had been slipped under Eliza's kitchen door. "I swear I will call the State Department and get her extradited if she persists in creeping round my house in the night." Eliza read the letter in its entirety, and in a voice of emphatic drama: "'Expulsion and excommunication are cruel and unusual punishments for the commission of a crime of which one has not been accused. I feel that I am living a Kafkaesque who-done-it that opens with my hanging as the criminal who has to double as the detective trying to discover my crime.' Here," said Eliza, "we come to our central mystery. Una writes, 'Was it the ice cream?' Una appears to suspect herself of having committed an ice cream. 'Give me five minutes'—three exclamation marks—'and I will tell you what I meant about consistency'—one more exclamation mark and a tearstain. 'Why will you not give me the opportunity to explain or maybe just plain apologize?' Tearstains. 'Of all the people I have ever met in all of my life . . .'" Eliza's voice suggested accompanying violins, "'I have never been so happy as in your and Leslie's company. . . .'" Eliza placed her right hand as if to hold up her left breast in the manner of certain neoclassic fountain statuary, and raised her eyes to the heavens above before lowering them onto page two: "'I have sat at your kitchen table and I have thought, There is no place in all the world where I would rather be than right here, right now.'"

Ilka was watching Winterneet walking toward her. Winterneet leaned against the wall beside Ilka, who said to him, "That's just how I feel about the Shakespeares' kitchen table."

"Me too, until Eliza goes on a tear."

Ilka experienced the small thrill of a small treachery. She said, "I am getting a bit weary of Eliza and the Una Wars."

"I," said Winterneet, "am getting out of town."

"How long do Eliza's tears usually last?"

"Until she finds the next old favorite to demolish. I'm going to London for the weekend," said Winterneet.

"No you're not, and I can prove it." Winterneet turned his face to look at Ilka, who said, "People I stand leaning against a wall at a party next to, don't go to London for weekends."

Winterneet said, "Come with me."

Ilka laughed and said, "That'll be the day!" and caught the sound—or caught the small, violent commotion, by her right ear—of Winterneet's face responding as if to one of those empty movie slaps. Ilka, unaware of having administered it, turned in surprise to see only the left ear, and slack left jaw, of Winterneet's face turning in a direction radically away from her. "A week in Copenhagen; a weekend in London!" said Ilka, who thought she was flattering the famous old man. "Sounds too damn glamorous."

"Does it?" Winterneet turned his face to look not at Ilka but straight before him. "It's a gas from the time I get out of bed in the morning until sometime around five in the afternoon. Then I want to die."

"Don't they give you receptions every night?"

"Every night," said Winterneet.

"Don't you get to meet everybody? You can have any damn body you want!"

"Evidently not," said Winterneet glumly.

Sunday Leslie beeped outside Ilka's gate. Eliza was fit to be tied. "Winterneet has taken Una to London with him."

"Really! He really took her? I didn't think he was serious!" Ilka would have liked Leslie to ask her what she was talking about. Ilka would have liked Leslie to know that Winterneet had invited her to come to London. She said, "Have you ever retrospectively understood what you didn't see while it was happening in front of your nose?"

But Leslie was turning into his drive and pulled up sharply. "Oh, for goodness' sake." In the middle of the driveway stood three cardboard boxes. Leslie said, "You go in and talk to Eliza." He got out, picked up the first of the boxes, and carried it into the house and up the stairs to his study.

Eliza said, "I'm fit to be tied."

"I think," Ilka said, "that traveling solo is Winterneet's memento mori. No one can bear being alone except most people keep right on bearing it. Winterneet can't, and he doesn't have to."

"Must be why every time he left the latest wife he moved in with us, bringing another box full of papers." She smiled blackly at Leslie who walked in rather out of breath. "We moved two boxes of his to Amherst with us, stored three with our things when we went back to Oxford, and now brought them to Concordance. For fifteen years Winnie has been going to take his boxes home as soon as he sorts through what he is going to throw away."

"Which he will never do, because" said Ilka, "the papers we are always going to throw away are the papers we are never going to read again, and we won't know which they are till we've read them again."

"That's so," said Leslie and looked at Ilka with the pleasure with which he looked at his wife when she said something that was true or funny.

Eliza said, "And Winnie might embarrass himself by coming across the Nobel Prize acceptance speech he wrote when he was twenty-three." Eliza's voice scratched like a saw moving up and down her throat.

Leslie uncrossed his right leg from over his left knee and crossed his left over his right leg. He said, "Dear."

"You know what Winnie did on the day we lost the baby?" Leslie rose and went to stand behind her. "He got out of town! The Bernstines to all intents and purposes moved in with us," Eliza said. "The Bernstines sat with us and howled with us and talked with us and were silent with us, and Winnie got out of town."

Ilka said, "Some of us don't know what to do around our friends when something terrible happens to them."

Eliza said, "I haven't called my friend Sarah, who wrote to tell me her son has leukemia."

"I wrote her," said Leslie.

"The hell you did," said Eliza swiveling her chair to give Leslie a pretend kick in the shins. Maybe it was not pretend.

Ilka said, "You can't mention what has happened in case you draw blood and you can't not mention it."

"Well Winnie," said Eliza, "doesn't like blood, so he got out of town and let it flow behind him."

"Dear," Leslie said, "that will do."

Ilka had supper with the Shakespeares Wednesday and the Bernstines dropped by. Jenny looked worriedly at Eliza and said, "Winnie's back. He's installed Una in his house."

Joe, looking sheepish, said, "We've offered Una an internship."

Several subjects were started and dropped into the abyss of Eliza's silence, so it seemed out of left field that she presently said, "Will no one take my part? Nobody is on my side? Leslie chauffeurs Una around town. Joe gives her a job. Ilka imagines her point of view; Ilka imagines Winnie's point of view. Ilka imagines everybody's point of view except mine."

Ilka said, "I'm doing sympathetic magic: I think what I think is that if I argue Una's and Winnie's points of view, someone, when you have had enough and dropped me, will argue my point of view." Ilka, who had thought that she was joking, discovered that she was going to cry.

"We are your elective cousins," said Leslie

"What do you plan to do for which you will deserve to be dropped?" asked Eliza.

"That," said Ilka, "is what I want you to promise that you will tell me."

Eliza said, "Make you a deal: If you'll quit imagining everything and everybody and making me look like the wicked witch of Concordance, I promise to bad-mouth you to your face."

"And Leslie, do you promise?"

The best that Leslie's conscience would suffer him to do was to offer to open another bottle of this quite nice white wine.

Crime

GARBAGE THIEF

This was back in the days when Ilka Weisz was new at the Concordance Institute. She had been at the Shakespeares' with colleagues and once for an institute dinner, but it excited her to enter their kitchen with them, by way of the garage. She tried to keep out of the way while they passed each other to reach the icebox and fix the drinks. They walked into the living room where Eliza said, "Leslie! The garbage thief!" and went to the window and banged on it. "Leslie!"

Leslie had sat down on the couch. Ilka wanted to go and sit beside him but she went and stood beside Eliza who was pummeling the glass. "What our Mrs. Coots calls 'the element,'" Eliza said. The garbage thief was a black man dressed in layers of black and dust, tall and thin, a pin head with a pronounced Adam's apple

and no chin. Ilka had expected an old bum but the garbage thief
was a young man. His long length curved into an "S" over the
Shakespeares' garbage with soft knees, whipping on the balls of
his feet in rather the way Eliza, in her kitchen, bent over her cutting and chopping. The man leaned suddenly all the way into
the can.

"He's thorough," Ilka said.

The young man stirred with a two-armed motion bringing the
things at the bottom of the garbage can to the surface. Large or
opaque objects which might hide treasure below he threw over
the sides.

"On my sidewalk!" said Eliza.

It's not your sidewalk, is what Ilka wanted to, but did not, say.

"Call the police."

Ilka did not say, He's not doing anything illegal! This was in
the early, wooing days of the friendship between Ilka and the
Shakespeares, and Eliza was older than Ilka by some fifteen years
and the Director's Wife.

"You threw out your pigskin driving gloves?" Eliza said to
Leslie.

"The left glove. I lost the right one."

"What if you find it?"

"That's what you said last year. Eliza, come and sit down."

"Sanitation is never going to pick up the mess!"

"I will pick up when he's gone."

"And I will help you," Ilka said.

The Shakespeares' street was lined with venerable, large, and
healthy trees. The sidewalk buckled with the upthrust of their
giant roots.

"Why don't you *not* come out?" Leslie said to Eliza and took
the broom out of her hands. "Messes make Eliza unhappy," he
explained to Ilka.

"Sunday's Book Review, Wednesday's pasta primavera," said Eliza.

"An argument against relativity," Leslie said. "What is healthy smells like itself; messes smell of corruption."

Ilka said, "When I was fifteen I bit into a moldy apple turnover. The probability of ever again meeting a moldy turnover is minimal, yet I've never bitten into another. And I love apple turnovers."

"Don't you loooove insights?" Eliza said. "There's Mother's brown teapot. Una broke the lid. Mother got it from our junk man. Our junk man worked our street first Monday of the month. Little brown horse, drum lamp shades stacked one inside the other, leprous fur coats, tennis racquets with no strings. Mother pointed and the junk man pulled out a brass candlestick. Mother said, 'What am I going to do with a single candlestick, unless you want to throw in—what are those legs sticking out—no, further back, on the left—right there. I could use a side chair.' Good little Bentwood. Mother had an eye. The garbage thief rejects my slippers."

"Why don't you go on inside?" Eliza had retired the three steps up the porch and stood holding her skirt in the classic stance of the female in the presence of small rodents. The squirrel sat up on its hind quarters moving its teeth with the rapidity of machinery.

"It's eating the crust from Sunday's deep-dish apple pie," said Eliza.

"Go away, shoo!" Leslie said to the squirrel. "You are meant to be frightened of me. You are meant to run away!" The animal registered the presence of the man with the broom by ceasing to nibble and sitting motionless.

Ilka said, "Human beings can't hold still like that!" The humans held still enough for the animal to come out of its freeze. It advanced on rapid feet as if wheels propelled it, froze, advanced and froze inches from Leslie's shoe. He had to stand with his feet together for fear of treading on the little beast. "Go away. Shoo." When he shook the broom the squirrel's fur waved like grass in the backdraft of a taxiing airplane. The three humans shared a sense of something mildly sinister. "It's mortally afraid of me but won't go away. I'll call campus security about the garbage thief."

This was before Ilka had a car of her own and Leslie offered to drive her home. "Come with us," he begged Eliza.

"No thank you. Drive *around* the project," she said to him.

Leslie had driven Ilka through the project, saying "The project makes Eliza unhappy." Ilka refrained from saying, Eliza's unhappiness is not the problem here, though contradiction was her instinct, her autobiography, her politics. Mention a fact and Ilka's mind kicked into action to round up the facts that disproved it. Express an opinion and Ilka's blood was up to voice an opposite idea. The day was not far when Ilka would begin to argue with Leslie and Eliza Shakespeare.

The project was an old, low-rise complex covering four square blocks and separated from Concordance University by the South Meadow. "In its day, it was a model of its kind," said Leslie.

"Why is the grass all chewed up? Why do the trees look as if they're on welfare? Why do they steal their own bricks out of their own walls?"

"Joe wants to fund a project project."

"They seem to be having a good time." Ilka meant the men talking in groups, boys and girls sitting on the walls, poking each other; a woman watered a corner garden of hollyhocks and tomatoes.

Leslie said, "Come on Sunday and help me get Eliza to go to the annual Summer Fiesta."

———

The fiesta was traditionally held on the Concordance campus. Ilka walked into the noise and commotion with the Shakespeares. "Why am I feeling cheerful?"

"Because it's summer," suggested Leslie.

"Seems silly to be happy because the sun's out."

"I don't have that problem," said Eliza.

"It's your wine," Ilka said. "It was the lovely lunch." She had held the pale golden soup in her mouth to check a taste different from any taste that she had ever known. "Cumin," said Eliza. Eliza's salad glistened more deeply green than regular salad. "Spinach," said Eliza.

Ilka had waited for them at their front door, listening to married people getting themselves out of their front door: keys were found where they were not supposed to have been left; ground-floor windows had not been locked. "The element will be out in force today," said Eliza. "Drive *around* the project."

"All right," said Leslie. Ilka said nothing.

"Leslie, park behind the institute. We have new hubcaps. God Almighty, what would the first president have said to barbecuing on his front lawn—The grass will never be the same."

Now Ilka said, "Bad for the grass, nice for the human beings."

Eliza said, "Puerto Ricans out in their Hawaiian duds."

Ilka said, "And the provost in his cricket whites, everybody walking together. It's the Peaceable Kingdom!"

"God Almighty!" Eliza said once more.

"And if he existed," said Ilka, "he would be in his heaven."

Here came the provost, a light, upright figure in white slacks and shirt, and his pleasant wife in chiffon with a modified garden hat, to pass the time of day with the new director of the institute and his formidable wife.

"We haven't had such a thoroughly splendid day for our fiesta since—" the provost mentioned a year within the present decade.

"What about . . ." said Eliza Shakespeare naming a random year. "That was fair to middling."

The provost's countenance held steady.

"As for—" and Eliza named yet another year, "that was a bummer."

Leslie introduced Ilka. "One of our junior members."

"Nineteen hundred sixty-nine," Eliza said, "that was another year."

"Well," said the provost. His wife aborted a squeak. The provost had pinched her, meaning "Start walking," forgetting she bruised easily.

"Let us hope and pray," Eliza said, "that next year will be—" and she mentioned the year that only doomsday could prevent it from being. "At least," Eliza said to the provost's diminishing back, "he keeps his shirt on. Why does the element want to run around naked?"

"Because the sun is out, " Leslie said.

Eliza said, "I'm going to bite the next person who mentions the weather. Hello, Bernstines. Hello, Teddy. Cassandra," she told the barking animal, "I know just how you feel."

"It's she saw a squirrel," Teddy said. Joe said, "Cassandra feels her responsibilities. There are dogs who smile. Cassandra frowns. Be glad, Cassandra! The sun is out, the sky is blue and everyone is walking together and eating and sitting on blankets. Cassandra, shut *up*! Did anybody see Bethy? Hello, Nat."

Nat Cohn was bent over a blanket on which an African student had spread neck chains, brooches, bangles, seeds, beads, small carved animals, chunks of amber.

"Ethnic, after a while, gets to all look the same," said Eliza. "Where's Nancy?"

"I wouldn't know," Nat said. "We are not talking."

The Bernstines walked off to look for Bethy. Joe said, "The Shakespeares have a new adoptee."

"I like Ilka," Jenny said and frowned anxiously.

———

Nat Cohn walked beside Ilka who said, "Hide me! There's Gerti Gruner from Conversational English. She keeps inviting me to supper and I never go, and there goes Sylvia Brandon. I invite her for a cup of coffee and she doesn't answer. She never remembers who I am."

Nat and Ilka had dropped a little behind. Nat said, "The Shakespeares have adopted you." The observation displeased Ilka. "We're friends."

"You and Leslie are friends."

Ilka said, "Leslie, Eliza, and I are friends."

"Yes, you are," Nat said. In a moment he added "I bet that at any given moment, in any room, you know Leslie's whereabouts, and whether he stands or sits, and who he's talking with, am I right?"

Ilka knew that she should deny the implication but it gratified her. "That's clever of you."

"I'm a very clever man," said Nat, "cleverer than Leslie. I'm the most empathetic man you have ever met. There's Nancy. I'm going to go so she can tell me how badly I am behaving. Maybe it's you and I who should be having that cup of coffee?"

Ilka caught up with the Shakespeares. "Nat is extraordinary. He walks into my head and tells me what I didn't know that I was thinking."

"Infernal cheek!" Eliza said. "Anybody walks into my head uninvited, I'd turf them out so fast!"

"It's sort of thrilling!" said Ilka.

"It's invasive," said Leslie unpleasantly.

"It's conversation," Ilka said.

Leslie said, "Conversation is not a sleight of hand, not a performance in which one shows off one's penetration at the expense of the other person. Conversation is a willing exchange of just as much as the participants are willing to expose to each other."

"Well, I think he's the best talker I have ever known. Why are you angry?"

"I'm not angry," said Leslie angrily.

Ilka looked to catch Eliza's eye but Eliza had spotted Bethy Bernstine. She said, "Like Jephtha's daughter wandering on the mountains."

"Do I know Jephtha's daughter?" asked Ilka.

"Jephtha won the Lord's battle after he promised to sacrifice the first thing that ran to meet him when he returned home, which, of course, happened to be not his puppy dog but his only daughter. 'Grant me two months,' Jephtha's daughter says, 'so that I may go and wander on the mountains and bewail my virginity, my companions and I,' and she departed, she and her companions, and bewailed her virginity in the mountains. Except Bethy has no companions. Hello, Bethy. Your father is looking for you. You have the kind of hair I want to get my hands into. Make your parents bring you round. I'm going to brush it for you. Hello Alicia! Alvin, don't go around looking so cheerful."

"We've come from the students' jazz combo, and they are *so* good."

"The Emperor's clothes," Eliza said. "The years I persuaded myself I liked jazz! If it just didn't have that thump thump."

"Dear Eliza!" said Alvin cheerfully. "There's Bach for you around the other side of the library."

The Shakespeares and Ilka went to find Bach. "There are the Zees," said Eliza waving. "Trust Maria to have a camp stool to sit on." The music was starting. When next Ilka looked, Eliza was transformed. Everything quick and malicious had drained out of the face she lifted to meet Bach in the air.

"What happened to Leslie?" Ilka and Eliza walked among the goods set out on trestle tables. "Carrot bread! Chhhh!" said Eliza. "Raw baking soda." She hissed at a display of pottery. "Why must we encourage the talentless to create. There he is." Among the toys on the next table, an electrified Santa raised his right arm simultaneously lowering his head with a sort of stammer, down, hesitate, down, stop. As the arm descended the head rose, hesitated, rose, stopped. Leslie Shakespeare, Director of the Concordance Institute, watched with head tilted and parted lips. Becoming aware of the two women watching him, he said, "I bought you a camp stool."

"Who is going to carry it?" asked Eliza.

"I will," said Leslie. "I bought it from our garbage thief. That's his table."

"Why is he wearing your Vayella shirt?"

"I gave it to him. It is too small for me."

"He takes our old junk and he sells it!"

Now Ilka said, "How wonderful! He makes use of things of no use to you."

"It's disgusting."

"It's entrepreneurship. The honorable profession of peddling. Some of my cousins peddled themselves into the American dream."

"You gave him my little green bucket?" Eliza said to Leslie.

"You said it leaked."

"We brought it from Amherst. That's a good roll of copper wire."

"Do we need copper wire?" asked Leslie.

"No. Mother would have liked the mahogany coat hangers the size of a man's shoulders. Don't come like that any more. Mother's teapot. Una broke the lid. When I asked my mother where she got me, she said, 'from the junk man.' She said she asked what he would take for the skinny baby in the bunting and the junk man had thrown me in with the spool-legged towel horse because she had bought a number of larger items that day—who could remember what all? I have the spool-legged towel horse in the upstairs bathroom."

——————

Nat called Ilka on the telephone. "Nancy and I have separated." Nat and Ilka had dinner in town.

"I told the Shakespeares you walk in and out of my head," Ilka reported, making mischief.

"And Leslie got huffy."

"Why should he get huffy?" asked Ilka. "When Jane Austen describes Mr. Knightly, one of the things she tells about him is that he is sensible. Leslie is a sensible man."

"And that turns you on," said Nat. "The beauty of common sense escapes women with less imagination."

"Oh, don't do that!" Ilka said. "Compliments aren't as much fun as everybody thinks."

"Then I will tell you some things you are no good at. You have no sense of direction, right."

"None. I don't understand maps. Was that a random guess?"

"You don't know which way to turn the clock at which time of year."

"I don't always know what year it is. Nat, do you have extrasensory perception?" she flattered.

"Extrasensory perception is nothing but observation past the point where the five senses tell you how things connect—the kind of thing you and I are more than ordinarily good at. So why don't you know why Leslie got huffy?"

The following week Nat moved back in with Nancy.

——————

A year had passed. The return of the garbage thief harbingered the Summer Fiesta. Leslie and Ilka looked through the living room window and saw Eliza with a broom staring at an object on the sidewalk. They went out to her.

Eliza said, "We don't eat porterhouse. This has got to be the Wentworths' next door." The three friends bent over what had been a beefsteak. Maggots recreated the shape they had eaten entirely away. The albino mass roiled internally. Each gyrating animal was held in place by the adjacence on its every side of others that precisely replicated it in motion, size, the absence of color or feature.

"Here we are then," said Eliza.

"It's fascinating!" Ilka bent closer. "Do they ever sleep? They're so vigorous—or desperate? What will they do now they've eaten up everything except each other? Where will they go?"

"Turn up in Yorick's skull," said Eliza.

"How do they know where to go? How do they know how to get there? Do they walk? In a phalanx? Single file?"

"It's your nitty gritty!" Eliza said.

"Eliza. It's not. It is really not," Leslie said to her.

"That one there—that's you," Eliza said to him. She pointed the broom.

"Eliza, come inside," said Leslie.

"This is Ilka. That one is me."

Leslie said, "Eliza, which one is Bach?"

"He's dead and the worms have eaten him. What I don't know is which one is the baby. The baby has to be somewhere. Do you understand that there has to be some one place where she has at any one moment got to be, alive or dead?" Leslie walked over and stood beside Eliza. Her hair stood away from her head. Her mouth was open in the square grin of one who has been touched by lightning.

Leslie took Eliza's elbow. She stumbled up the last step not having lifted her foot high enough to clear the riser. Leslie's hand guided her through the front door into the kitchen where she stood and seemed not to recognize the geography. Leslie led her to the table where she stood without an agenda. Leslie made her sit down.

Ilka, aghast, said, "Should I leave?"

"If you don't mind."

"Of course!"

Leslie said, "We have been here before. I know what to do."

AT WHOM THE DOG BARKS

A stock turn of phrase, "A poor man but honest."
Perhaps that's why the man is poor—because he is honest.
Why don't we say, "A rich man but honest?"

—Max Frisch

Down the Hatch

Who had swiped the Concordance Institute's electric pencil sharpener from the top of the file cabinet between the reception desk and the door to the conference room? Celie said, "Anybody could have walked out with it, and will they be disappointed! It never worked. I use my old hand crank."

"And you're right!" said Nat Cohn. "'Anybody' is plural. Not a thing Fowler can do about it."

"For goodness' sake, let's get ourselves a new electric sharpener," said Leslie Shakespeare and got out his wallet.

"Don't we want to know who done it?" asked Joe Bernstine.

"Mr. Winterneet popped in and out," Celie said. "He says to

say he's back in town and going straight to bed but he left these."
These were a couple of bottles of red wine.

Leslie studied them and said, "Let's have a party, or has everyone gone home?"

Celie said Alvin, Zachariah, and Yvette had left, but Ilka was in her office. Leslie said, "Everybody, bring your own glasses. I'll ring Eliza." Leslie carried the bottles to his office. Nat Cohn went to his office to call Nancy. Joe called Jenny. Jenny Bernstine brought Teddy who brought his dog, Cassandra, who was frowning and barking.

"Whatever you are trying to tell me," said Eliza, leaning her face down to the little dog's agitated nose, "maybe I don't want to know it."

"Cat spat at her," said Teddy.

The cat was the institute's tom. The institute's members had never resolved the philosophical difference between those who couldn't stomach animals with people names and those who could stomach none of the clevernesses that had been proposed instead. All the while, contended Nat Cohn, the cat grew more bitter.

"I'll put him in the mailroom if someone will remember to let him out. I'm leaving, O.K.?" said Celie.

"O.K., Celie. Thanks. Good night," everybody said.

Ilka watched Leslie Shakespeare sitting in the embrasure of the window, which opened onto the late summer garden at an angle that kept the newer brick and glass structures out of sight. Before him, in comfortable conversation, stood Joe Bernstine, who kept turning his head, shifting his weight, combing his fingers through his hair; he put out a hand to remove the curtain that the evening breeze had laid across his friend's shoulder. Eliza had taken the chair next to Ilka and said, "Joe, the Jewish jumping bean," which made Ilka jump. Ilka loved Eliza Shakespeare. Eliza in her three-dollar Woolworth shirt looked classy beside Nancy Cohn, who looked merely chic. Nancy stood by the darkening west window and glowered.

Jenny Bernstine, aware of the whereabouts, at any time, in any room, of her husband and her children, was sitting in Leslie's chair behind Leslie's desk. She said, "Teddy, you can't sit on Cassandra, darling, you're smothering her."

"It shuts her up," said Teddy.

"Only she's got to breathe, and, Teddy, take a comb to the poor thing! Anybody ever see a dog with hair that goes so every which way?"

"Who swiped my *Backyard Thief*?" asked Teddy.

"I did," said Nat Cohn. Nat sat reading, sunk way down in the old broken-backed armchair. The dense growth of Nat's hair and beard had connected itself in Ilka's mind with the undifferentiated bushiness of the surrounding Connecticut hillsides which she experienced as a subliminal disappointment on her morning drive to the institute: another night had failed to develop the local landscape into her childhood's Alps.

Nat said, "We don't write stories like this any more! Chronic plot deficiency is our problem. Forget the vitamins and get your daily dose of soap opera."

"I notice you never miss yours," said his wife.

"It's about there are these kids, Theo and Ellie," Teddy said, "and their dog is Cassandra, which is how come Cassandra got to be called Cassandra, that is going to be the police dog. This thief has stolen their dad's glasses and everything. Oh. I forgot, there's this big old policeman that is really dumb. His name is Drummond. And the parents go to bed. They go out in the yard and the children get mad because this squirrel runs up the tree and Cassandra doesn't stop barking and the dad comes down and puts Cassandra in the attic and they don't know the thief is all this time sitting in the tree. Oh and I forgot that . . ."

"Teddy, the crayons are in the bottom drawer in my office."

"My idea of hell," Eliza said in Ilka's ear, "is a child telling you the plot of a story."

Nancy Cohn said, "If you *have* to read while everybody else is sitting together and talking, at least turn on the goddamn light." It was when Nat reached to pull the chain made of little interconnected balls that should have turned on Leslie's standing lamp that everybody noticed the lamp wasn't there. Where was the lamp? Who had swiped the standing lamp out of Leslie's office?

Leslie said, "I can imagine someone walking the electric pencil sharpener out of the front door, but not a five-foot standing lamp."

"The electric sharpener? I took it to be fixed," said Jenny Bernstine. "It never really worked."

The solution of one mystery activates the sanguine part of the mind to expect the next mystery—that mysteries as such are able to be solved. The fact is that nobody ever saw Leslie's lamp again. There was no response to the memo requesting that whoever had borrowed the director's standing lamp out of the director's office please return it, no questions asked, which Leslie's assistant, Wendy, Xeroxed on the copier downstairs in the mailroom the morning after the wine party in Leslie's office. Coming up the stairs, Wendy handed Celie a copy and continued down the corridor into the lounge, where she put a memo into each of the pigeonholes for the fellows, associates, staff, and maintenance people. Celie went up to Leslie's office. "Why don't I copy a bunch and post them on the trees around the campus?"

"Good idea," Leslie said.

Celie went down to the mailroom and came hollering up the stairs. The copier was gone. Leslie had front and back doors locked. He asked everybody in the building to come into the conference room to meet with Officer Right and his partner.

"Teddy, go get the crayons," Joe said. Jenny had dropped the little boy and his dog off to go shopping with Bethy.

"Daddy, Cassandra says please please please!" Cruel to be sent away when there was a real thief and *two* live policemen!

"O.K., but, Teddy, if you can't keep that animal quiet, you're out of here, both of you."

"I'll sit on her."

"And you be quiet, or I'll sit on you!"

Officer Right asked if there was any history of theft at the institute. He was a weighty, elderly policeman and looked as if he knew what he was doing. "Anything—big, small?"

Joe said, "Nothing I know of since Edwin, our first fundraiser—man I went to school with!—absconded with the funds he raised for us, and that's fifteen odd years ago. Then, yesterday, the five-foot standing lamp disappears from the director's office. Today our new copier walks out of our mailroom!"

"Been bad all over," Officer Right's partner, Juan Jose, said, "with the project right the other side of South Meadow."

Ilka could leave it to Alvin, the institute's radical, to say, "Because the city council pockets the money they themselves, mind you, allocated to the project," to which Zachariah, the institute's conservative, responded, "It's not the city council that walked in and walked off with our copier," and Alvin said, "No, the project walked in and walked out with our copier."

Leslie said, "Please . . ."

"Where was the copier?" asked Officer Right.

"In the mailroom right underneath us, which used to be the kitchen when the room we're sitting in was the dining room of the first president's residence."

Teddy said, "And if you pull that chain next the dumbwaiter, this little tab thing that says 'd-i-n-i-n-g-r' wobbles down in the mailroom."

"Teddy . . ."

"Let's take a look," Officer Right said.

"Can I Daddy, can I show him, Daddy, can I . . ."

"You can come down with us so long as I don't know you're there."

The whole group walked down the stairs into the mailroom. The cat, sitting on the ledge over the dumbwaiter, hissed and pointed his tail to the heavens, and Cassandra went into a paroxysm of barking, leaping, and snapping long after the enemy had streaked out the door and up the stairs. "Stop it! Come on, Cassandra!" Teddy kept saying.

Joe said, "Take the dog into my study!" in a voice there was no arguing with. "This is the table the copier stood on," he told the policeman. "There used to be one of those great black stoves we should never have got rid of."

"Does this basement have an exit to the outside?"

Celie said, "The only exit is the stair you came down on, right across from my desk that's across from the front door."

"Could someone have slipped up the stairs while you went up to talk to Director Shakespeare about posting notices on trees?"

"Teddy! *Into* my office and close the door," Joe called to the top of the stairs where Cassandra leaped, barked, and barked and barked and barked.

Celie said, "No, because, Barbara . . ."

"That's me," said the librarian.

". . . was coming out of the kitchen with a cup of coffee . . ."

"Tea," said the librarian.

". . . and I asked her to sit at my desk till I got back. I took the elevator up . . ."

"Where's the elevator?"

"Across from the reception desk," Celie and Barbara said with one voice.

"And you took the elevator from the second floor straight down to the mailroom?

"And the copier was gone."

"What I want to know," said the officer, "is *how* he could have walked the thing out of the mailroom."

Alpha, the institute's feminist, said, "Why do you assume the thief was male?"

"How much would you say the copier weighs?"

The guesses quarreled with each other.

Alpha said, "She could have heaved it onto the dolly we use for hauling boxes of papers."

But there stood the dolly, underneath the dumbwaiter hatch, where it always stood.

Leslie said, "Do I understand you to think that the copier might still be in the building?"

"That the thief might still be in the building," said Officer Right.

"And we may have gone to school with him," Alvin gleefully hoped.

"That dog has got to go," Joe said to Leslie as they trooped back up the stairs and heard the helpless barking, and Cassandra burst out of his office, straining toward the stairs.

What was Cassandra looking for in the mailroom? Why did she bark all the way home? Joe locked her into the spare room upstairs. The experience appeared to have driven the little dog insane: what would you have done if all you knew was how to bark and you knew that a cat sitting and spitting on the ledge over the dumbwaiter hatch didn't mean the answer was not inside?

It wasn't till the next evening, when Ahmed, the institute's janitor, went into the mailroom to turn out the lights, that he heard the rasping of chains and a creaking inside the dumbwaiter. It had not been in use for decades past. His wrestling the hatch door open might have caused the wooden platform to give way and tilt the institute's copier into the space below. By this time, of course, the thief was long gone and the members of the institute were free to feel reinforced in thinking that he, or she, must have been one of the greedy rich, alternatively one of the hapless poor, both of whom we have always had and always will have among us.

In the upstairs spare room Cassandra barked and barked and barked and barked and barked.

Supermarket

On Sunday, when Ilka came to brunch at the Shakespeares', Eliza had her Supermarket Adventure to relate: Eliza said she had run in and made straight for household items, imagining the policeman waiting by her car with a parking ticket. "I scanned those clever little packaged items, found my spatula, raced to the checkout: long, long line. Woman in front of the woman in front of me had a full basket. In 10 Items or Less! It's a wicked world. The woman with the full basket wrote out the slowest check in history. I imagined myself telling the policeman, 'I thought, officer, parking was legal around this corner!' and I imagined *you*," Eliza said to Leslie, "saying, 'Dear, but that is not the truth!' and imagined the pleasure of kicking you in the shins." Ilka was studying Leslie. He was concentrating on the management of an overripe peach.

"The checkout girl," continued Eliza, "called for a manager to O.K. the check. No manager in sight, of course. The checkout girl walked away to look for the manager and I walked out of the supermarket with my sixty-nine-cent spatula, raced to my car which was standing, quiet as could be, illegally, where I had parked it. I'm wanting to get out of there. Where are my car keys? Where is my handbag? It is not slung over my right shoulder where it is supposed to be. *Now,* I remember the girl from the project standing in the line behind me."

Ilka and Eliza were friends in the habit of arguing. Eliza had to know this was going to activate Ilka. Ilka asked Eliza how she knew the girl was from the project.

Eliza said, "She was black."

"How do you know the black girl took your handbag?"

"Because when I walked into the checkout line I had my handbag slung over my shoulder and when I got outside I didn't have it."

"Eliza! Eliza, you don't know the girl took it!"

"So where is it? Where are my keys? Where is my wallet with my money, credit cards, driver's license?"

"Eliza! Leslie!" pleaded Ilka, "don't you have to presume the girl innocent till proven guilty . . ."

But Leslie stood at the sink with his back to both women, washing his hands clean of peach juice.

"'Innocent till proven guilty!' Interesting idea," said Eliza and added, "Why don't you stay? The Bernstines and the Stones are coming over."

"Wonderful!" said Ilka.

Ilka thought of the saying *Teaching your grandmother to suck eggs* and it made her blush. Ilka had half a notion that Eliza had invented the black girl and the lost handbag to get a rise out of her, when a tidy old black man with a bicycle rang the doorbell: He had found Eliza's handbag. The wallet was gone.

"Usually they take the money, and leave the wallet with the papers that you don't want them to find on you. Good thing they left your library card with your name. Me—I used to pickpocket but I didn't have the nerve. It's like everything else: I went into this business. I don't look in the residential cans—people's yesterday's dinners is disgusting. I do mostly Main Street and the malls. People are glad to have their handbags, whatever they feel it's worth it to them."

Leslie gave the man a five dollar bill and asked him, "So, is it a living?"

"It's like everything else: it depends. Got one more this side of town, and one on North Street. You have a nice day now."

"Thank you," said Eliza, "But I have other plans."

The Stones were first to arrive and Alfred was helping Leslie bring chairs out onto the front lawn when the Bernstines arrived. They'd had to bring Cassandra who was driving the neighborhood crazy. "It's like everything else," Eliza said. Joe took the dog upstairs and locked her into one of the bedrooms.

Eliza related her Supermarket Adventure. When she got to the part where she walked out with the sixty-nine-cent spatula, Ilka said, "I once stole a roast beef." Everybody was impressed. Ilka said, "The price tag had come off and the checkout girl said I had to take it back and get another. The meat department was way in the back. I could feel the people in the line behind me breathing, so I said, 'Forget it.' The girl checked me through, and then she told me to take the roast beef back to the meat department. I had my bag of groceries in one hand, the roast beef in the other and I walked out of the store. What I want to know," she said to Eliza, "is why you are so sure it was the girl in the check-out line who stole your handbag."

Eliza said, "'Will you walk a little faster said the whiting to the snail. There's a porpoise close behind me and he's treading on my tail.' I had to take a step backward to make this girl take a step back. She stole my handbag."

"It's chemistry," Dr. Alfred Stone said. "We've done experiments with magpies. Take ten birds. Tag five and inject them with an antikleptin. Put shiny odds and ends in a box. The unmedicated birds dive into the box and fly the things back into their cages. The tagged birds sit there. Crime is chemical."

"Unless chemistry is moral, too," mused Leslie.

"How," argued Ilka, "could the girl take a bag that was slung over your shoulder and you not know it!"

"Beats me," said Eliza. "Yes? What is it?" she called to the black woman standing outside the wrought-iron gate. The woman was saying "Psst, psst" to attract the attention of the party on the chairs on the grass. She wore a cloth coat that looked too warm for the mild evening. A little girl, some seven or eight years old, climbed onto the gate and stood peering over it. Ilka watched Leslie's back move down the path. The child jumped off the gate and hid behind the woman's coat. Ilka watched Leslie come back up the path. He said, "She found your keys."

"That's nice, but we already changed our locks."

"Come and talk with her, Eliza."

The group on the lawn chatted while Leslie and Eliza talked with the woman at the gate. Leslie broke off a stem of red cherry tomatoes and gave it to the little girl. The woman and the child left. Eliza and Leslie came back. Eliza said, "One gives little girls cookies, not tomatoes!"

They sat down. The little girl stood outside the gate. "Come in! Come here!" Leslie called, but the little girl ran away.

The woman was back, going "Psst, psst." She had found two of Eliza's credit cards. The woman went away.

The woman and the little girl stood at the gate and had found Eliza's empty wallet.

The woman and the child went away and a girl stood at the gate.

"That's her." Eliza said.

"If that's the girl who took your bag she wouldn't come and stand at your gate!" argued Ilka, but at her upstairs window Cassandra leaped and leaped. They could hear the faint, hectic sound of her barking. Eliza went to talk to the girl at the gate.

"Where do you live?" Eliza asked her.

"In the project. My neighbor," said the girl, "thought you would give her a reward."

"I would," said Eliza, "but someone has taken my money."

Main Street

Ilka looked into Leslie's office shortly before noon. "You might want to check your home phone. Your line's been busy all morning."

Leslie grinned. "Eliza made a deal with the girl. Eliza promised not to call the police if the girl came and made the telephone calls to cancel Eliza's credit cards. Punishment to fit the crime."

"The girl confessed that she took the bag!"

"No."

There was something in Ilka which believed that other people, if properly argued with, could not but think as she, Ilka, thought. "Leslie," she pleaded, "I believe that I might be able to continue living in this world if you will do me the incalculable favor of agreeing with me on a point the size of the head of a pin: acknowledge that you don't know if the black girl stole Eliza's handbag or not!"

Leslie said, "Betty, Barbara, and Celie were mugged coming out of the Pancake House after work yesterday. Barbara's elbow got scraped when the mugger dragged her along the sidewalk by the strap of her handbag, which had the institute keys in it. The locksmith is downstairs changing the locks. Barbara says he, or she, was chunky and wore jeans, a jeans jacket and a shower cap pulled over the face. Since when," cried Leslie, "do muggers mug three people walking down Main Street!"

The Middle of the Street

Officer Right advised women—advised everybody—to walk down the middle of the street. Officer Right had never in his years on the force known anybody to get mugged walking down the middle.

That night a mugger approached Alvin and Alicia walking down the middle of the street. He took Alvin's wallet and disappeared into the shadows of the sidewalk.

Walking back from babysitting, Bethy kept on the sidewalk; it was only a block and a half to her house. In the circle of light from the street lamp the small rain came down in oblique lines like the first stage of cross-hatching. Presently the child knew someone walked behind her. She walked faster and so did the other. He came so close that he could, like Alice in Wonderland's duchess, have hooked his chin over her shoulder. "Take me home," said his hoarse whisper as if inside Bethy's own ear. She turned fiercely on the face inches from her own—sick eyes, dripping stubble. The man was no taller than herself. He had drawn his head down between his shoulders in the forlorn hope that this might keep him from getting wetter. "Go away," barked the terrified girl. The man said, "Oh, O.K.," and backed into the black and the rain coming down really hard now.

Bethy deduced that the wet bum had not really liked her. She told nobody.

On Campus

Yvette was mugged on campus at broad noon.

A man in a baseball cap asked her the way to the library. Yvette pointed out the stone building behind the glass building. The man in the baseball cap said, "I'll take your pocketbook. What's in the paper bag?"

"Apples," Yvette said. "I'll take the apples," said the man. Yvette saw Officer Juan Jose and yelled and the man in the cap ran away almost knocking down Ilka who was coming in by the

South Gate. "He shoved me," she reported. "I don't think I ever experienced anything as powerful as this wanting to get away. It was kind of fascinating."

"Was he white?" asked Eliza

"What's that got to do with it?" yelled Ilka.

"What is going on!" said Leslie. "What happened to thieves doing what they do decently under cover of night!"

The Bernstines' Bedroom

It was in the night that a thief came into the Bernstines' bedroom. Cassandra had been barking and barking, Joe reported in the institute kitchen the next morning. "All we did was curse her and try and go back to sleep. Officer Right says the thief squeezed the plastic accordion together and got in between the air conditioner and the window frame."

"He was so thin!" said Jenny Bernstine.

"How do you know?"

"Because he turned on the light."

"The thief turned the light on?" cried Leslie.

"To see what there was to steal, I guess. My gold bracelet was on the dressing table—Cassandra, the thief is gone! Have a heart, Cassandra, you're among friends here!"

"Never send to ask at whom the dog barks," said Ilka, "she barks at me. The roast beef!"

"That wasn't stealing," Eliza said, "because you didn't need it."

Cassandra barked at Eliza: the sixty-nine-cent spatula.

"I was in a hurry. And maybe dogs don't know the little thrill of getting something for nothing," said Eliza.

"What about the thrill of getting something when you've got nothing," shouted Ilka.

Cassandra barked at Leslie, who said, "Oh, Cassandra, that's a long time ago," and, surprisingly, blushed.

Cassandra barked at Teddy. Perhaps he had got his hands in the cookie jar or because he was choking her.

Cassandra barked at her own front paws, gnawed and chewed at the fur between her toes, and barked and barked and seemed never to be going to stop.

A GATED COMMUNITY

Celie called the members in their offices: Leslie wanted everybody in the conference room, spouses welcome since it affected the whole community.

"You all know Officer Right from Security. I'd like you to meet Mr. Charley who comes to us from the Planning Commission. You all know Marvin." Marvin was the institute's lawyer. "Marvin is going to check into the options in light of the neighborhood situation . . ."

"We have a situation?" Alvin said.

"The garbage situation," Eliza said.

"Parking on campus," said Zack Zee.

"The project."

"Why is the project a situation?"

"Drug rings," said Zack.

"Please!" said Leslie. "We're talking about a sudden wave of crime. The standing lamp disappears from my office, the copier walks itself into the mailroom hatch, Betty and Barbara are mugged coming out of the Pancake House and so are Alvin and Alicia walking down the middle of the street! A robber squeezes past the Bernstines' air conditioner and turns the light on! Yvette is robbed on campus at noon."

"The girl from the project steals my wallet," Eliza added.

"You don't know that," said Ilka.

Ahmed was arranging the stand for Mr. Charley's charts and maps. "You're fortunate," said this gentleman, "that Concordance University, originally conceived as the Concordance School for Higher Women, was a gated community. There's still a quarter mile of wall here, on the right side of Southgate, and another hundred feet here." The Man from the Planning Commission flipped to a new map, "and here and here."

"A wa-all!" said Alvin, Alpha, Ilka, and the two Bernstines on a descending note. "A wall?" mused Zack, Maria, Yvette and Eliza Shakespeare with rising interest.

The lawyer said, "Leslie wants me to look into the charter. The city might have been liable for the upkeep of the wall for half a century. The city might be liable for rebuilding."

"A wall is a thought!"

"We're not having a wall!"

"You put a layer of cement on it and embed broken glass," said Officer Right.

"Keep Una out," said Eliza.

"Dear," said Leslie. To the members he said, "I would urge that we allow our experts to explain our options which we can discuss at leisure on our own time."

The Man from Planning said, "You'd have to reinstate the old gatehouse."

"How many guards would it take on a twenty-four-hour basis?" wondered Leslie.

"At the time it was built"—the Man from Planning turned to a large scale map—"it would have enclosed only the buildings erected before 1910—the library, Philosophy Hall, the President's residence which is now Concordance Institute, and the South Meadow—but you might want to include the streets adjacent to the university as well."

"Keep out the garbage thief," said Eliza.

"Permanently padlock the smaller access gates here, here, and here, creating a series of dead-end streets. It would solve the parking problem around the campus."

"How would the folks from the project get to Concordance Supermarket?" asked Alvin.

"It would solve the parking problem," said Maria Zee.

"Why couldn't they go around to the west, or go east to the Bottom Dollar Market?" Eliza Shakespeare said.

"It would solve the parking around campus," Zack Zee said.

"What's involved?" Leslie asked the Man from Planning.

"You would need to zone access and parking. Have city planning call an all-agency conference: the housing authority; management and maintenance; the department of streets; the keeper of the official map, tenant selection policy and defensive architecture dedicated streets restricted and controlled entry. You have to de-map the mapped streets and deed them to the city, fenced guarded locked at sundown privately accessed in return for easement of utilities, but check your minimum maintenance contracts with fire sanitation and police or you might find yourselves minus municipal services, without water, outside the postal zone, and nobody picking up your garbage."

"*Something* has got to be done about the project," Zachariah Zee said.

"I always wanted to fund a project project," Joe said.

"Get the city fathers to cough up the funds for the upkeep," said Alvin.

"What they'd like is to turn it into middle-income housing," said the Man from Planning.

Zack Zee said, "Drug rings."

"Parking," Maria said.

"The garbage thief," Eliza Shakespeare said.

"What's wrong with picking something up for nothing and peddling it for something!" Ilka shouted.

"It makes a mess on the sidewalk," Eliza said. "They take their shirts off," she said. "The grass will never be the same."

Parking, garbage, the garbage thief, drug rings, robberies at noon, walls, no walls. No glass embedded in cement, they argued back in Leslie's office after Officer Right, Marvin the lawyer, and the Man from Planning had left.

Deaths

FATAL WISH

"Do you want me to disqualify myself," Ilka asked Director Leslie Shakespeare, "because I know Jimmy?"

The members of the Concordance Institute continued turning the pages of the candidate's vita on the table before them, but their ears pricked up. The young man was understood to have stayed the night in Ilka's little rented house, and they had been rather wondering.

Was Ilka sleeping with Jimmy Carl? Not any longer, and not yet.

Ilka had picked Jimmy up accidentally at her very first New York party to which she had come with another man with whom she had been falling in love. The man's name was Carter—a large, stout, distinguished black man, in his fifties, and ill. When he walked off to get his whiskey, Ilka stood and watched a be-spectacled man who held his head at an excruciating angle, pre-tending to be reading the spines of the books on the glass shelving. He was, like Ilka herself, young, thin, Jewish, and embarrassed. He appeared to be alone. It was because he did not attract her that Ilka had smiled at him, and because she wanted to practice her English that she asked him if he was a friend of the bride or the groom. The young man's brow contracted over his left eye, his nostrils dilated, his lips parted and he told Ilka the dates from and until which he and the groom had interned for which Washington congressman. Ilka was trying to remember whom the young man reminded her of—someone she didn't much care for. She said, "I must go and search my friend," but the young man had kept at her side and was never going to be lost again.

The first several times he called he had been obliged to iden-tify himself. "Jimmy Carl. Jimmy. Remember me from Philip and Fanny's wedding?"

He happened to call the day they took Carter away to the state hospital. Jimmy took Ilka to the corner Chinese restaurant. Ilka studied the oversized menu, looked up, and there, across the table from her, sat a young man! Jimmy Carl from Philip and Fanny's wedding! His left brow contracted, his nostrils dilated, his lips parted: Ilka leaned all her attentive interest and then some across the table so the young man would not notice that she had forgot-ten him.

Jimmy Carl had just got fired from his job. "The president called me into his office. The president is my mother's cousin."

"And he fired you!"

"He had his reasons. There's a man, Stackport—looks like he's got a case of permanent morning mouth. He files at the file next to my file. He files a file, he files another file, another file. I thought, I can go faster than that if I put the files on my lap, pick the top one up with my right hand while I get the next ready with my left, except that doesn't leave a hand to scratch one's nose with. Boredom is really interesting, actually: you have this stuffed head, pain between the shoulder, pins and needles in the right foot, your nose itches. I mean how do I know that that's boredom? This is two minutes to eleven! Ninety-two minutes before I get to meet you for lunch." Jimmy blushed. "I thought, if I file fifteen files without looking at the clock it'll be eleven. Then I thought, I'll file fifteen *more* files, and by then it'll already be two minutes *after* eleven! I look. Clock says it's *one* minute *to* eleven. Which is interesting. I've got as close as a human being gets to what eternity feels like: I can't imagine a minute that doesn't have an end, but I can imagine an endless number of minutes filing—a sneak preview of hell. Which is a fascinating concept for human beings to have come up to scare ourselves with. So I sort of tilt my head to rub my nose on my shoulder and feel my files going into a slide. Imagine an eternal moment of embarrassment: Mr. Stackport has stopped filing; Mrs. Winters—she's the office manager, really nice woman—she swivels her chair and looks at me; the typewriters stop; somebody giggles. Mr. Stackport is on his knees— which is sort of wonderful, really—an adult male in his sixties, children, grandchildren, I wouldn't wonder—takes home a fraction of what Cousin Robert makes, and he's red in the face because Cousin Robert's files are all over the office floor! He says, 'How come you didn't put a blue label on Kux, Bloch & Co? Kux, Bloch is inactive!' And Cousin Robert! He *really minded* the inactive files being filed in the drawer with the active files!"

"But that's awful—getting fired!"

"Yes. Well, no, actually, it was interesting. Poor Robert. I can talk rings around Cousin Robert."

———

Carter came out of the hospital and went back into the hospital. Jimmy got a junior job writing reports for the American Civil Liberties Union, from which he did not get fired. Why was Ilka surprised? Jimmy said the reports were interesting. And whenever Carter was in trouble, Ilka called Jimmy Carl and they had long conversations. It was Jimmy who came to the station with Ilka, finally, to see Carter off to the West Coast.

For a time Ilka and Jimmy slept together. Jimmy was a friendly, enthusiastic lover. Ilka was surprised that inside his narrow suit he was nicely put together. It wasn't his fault that her arms and heart were used to encompassing more bulk. When Jimmy got transferred to the office of the ACLU in Washington, he was shocked to understand that Ilka was not coming with him. His left brow frowned, his nostrils flared, his lips parted and he said, "Interesting how impossible it is to really believe one isn't going to get something one wants!"

Ilka suddenly asked him if he had ever been on TV.

"Once. When I was a student at Columbia. One of those conscientious Sunday-morning dialogues."

"You sat on the left," Ilka said.

"This is weird. This is incredible! I mean this is way before I even knew you!"

"I can't remember what it was about," said Ilka. What Ilka remembered was that the boy on the left, who turned out after all those years to have been Jimmy Carl, said all the things that Ilka herself would have said, and that they sounded tiresome. While the boy on the right spoke, the camera had panned to the disagreement expressed by the left boy. His face had taken up the screen, squared off above the left-sided frown and below the lips drawn apart by the unlucky trick the muscles of the cheek played on the wings of the nose. Ilka swore it in her heart: Jimmy would never, never, never know that years before she met him, Ilka had got out of bed and walked over to the television and turned Jimmy off.

"Why won't you marry me?" whined Jimmy whenever he flew in from Washington.

"Because," Ilka routinely answered, "you don't ask me if I will but why I won't."

"So will you?"

"Don't be silly."

Jimmy then told Ilka what was wrong with his latest Washington date, and Ilka was bemused to diagnose in herself the ghost of jealousy. Ilka tended to like the women Jimmy brought to New York to meet her, and to be surprised that these conversable women should like Jimmy, till she remembered that she, Ilka, liked Jimmy. Over the next several years Jimmy expanded. The shoulders gained in consequence. There was more *of* Jimmy front to back. Why was Ilka surprised when Jimmy began to publish his articles and essays?

At a certain time after Ilka received her appointment as a junior associate at the Concordance Institute and moved to Connecticut, Jimmy phoned. He'd seen the institute's ad for a director of projects. How would Ilka feel if he applied?

"But you like it at the ACLU."

"Why wouldn't I love it at the Concordance Institute?"

"Jimmy, what do you know about developing conferences? What do you know about organizing things? And what do you know about 'Who's Who in Scholarship'?"

"Zilch, zilch, and zilch," said Jimmy.

When Jimmy drove up from Washington to be interviewed, the Shakespeares had a reception for him. From across the room Ilka watched Leslie introduce Jimmy around, saw Jimmy's brows contract and his nostrils dilate, and walked out into the kitchen.

"We like your friend," Eliza Shakespeare said.

"You do?" marveled Ilka.

"He lives such an interesting life," Eliza said. "At the moment of his death Jimmy will be thinking, Fascinating concept—dying!"

Leslie said, "I like Jimmy. He talks a lot like you do."

"I know it!" cried Ilka, "I know," and understood that it was herself whom, at that wedding to which Carter had taken her, Jimmy had reminded her.

Ilka took Jimmy to a party at Martin Moses's. Jimmy drove, Ilka held the map. "I was at a party at his house once, but there *is* no DeKalb Avenue this side of town."

"DeKalb Street?"

"No DeKalb Street. Maybe this map is wrong. The road we're on doesn't have a name."

"Has to have a name."

"Has no signs. Carter used to say they don't want you to know. If you belonged there you would know the name of the street. If you don't belong, go away. He said in the war, the British took down the street signs to confuse the enemy."

Jimmy stopped the car. "What's the number of this house?"

"It doesn't have a number."

"Could you get out and take a look?"

Ilka came back and reported, "They don't want us to know the number." There was a light on in an upstairs window. "There must be a person. Ilka, go and ring the bell." The upstairs light went out. A light had came on downstairs. The person must have walked down the stairs. "That's so interesting," Jimmy said, "people in houses everywhere leaving one room to go into another room to do what?"

"Tidy up? Sit down? Look for something they have lost?"

"A book. A phone number."

"That might be the kitchen. To look what's in the refrigerator?"

"Go and ring the bell and ask where the hell we are."

Ilka walked up the path and the three steps. She rang the bell and peered through the frosted glass at an approaching person acquiring size and bulk. The person turned the handle inside on the inside of the door and opened. It was Gerti Gruner, who said, "You have come!"

It would be dastardly to stand in the way of a friend's career because one preferred to have him in Washington. Recognizing the conflict of her interest, Ilka had asked Leslie if she should disqualify herself.

"Oh, I don't think so," replied Leslie. "What do you say, Joe?"

"I say that you and I didn't disqualify ourselves from co-opting each other."

"Zack?" Leslie said.

Zack said, "What makes this candidate think he knows how to run projects like ours?"

"Nobody knows how to run projects like ours," said Alvin.

"I pass Alvin in the corridor and there's this cheerful whoosh," Ilka had said to the Shakespeares at Sunday breakfast in Eliza's kitchen which was suffused with green garden light.

Eliza had said, "It comes from believing the world is going to shape up, and Alvin knows the shape it ought to be. Alvin knows the revolution that would do it if Zachariah weren't standing in the way. Poor Zack! His nose grows right in the middle of his face."

Ilka and Leslie laughed. "That's true! It does!" they said.

Leslie said, "You leave Zack alone. I never hear better sense than I do from Zachariah."

"He has a mouth like a keyhole," said Eliza.

Ilka grieved at the prospect, if Jimmy got hired, of having to share the Shakespeares and Eliza's kitchen. "Will there be a battle?"

"Yes," said Leslie.

"I haven't been here long enough to understand what's behind what everybody says," Ilka said. "I wish somebody would tell me the stories of all the skeletons."

Leslie said, "I don't know what has been happening here for the last ten and more years, but I bet you'd be disappointed. The skeletons are not sinister."

"And yet they reach their hands out of their closets and determine everything that everybody argues and how everybody votes."

"That's probably true."

"Anyway," Ilka had said, "we're all of us guaranteed to do our usual numbers."

Alvin's number, at Monday morning's meeting, was to get young Jimmy on board, Zachariah's was to hold the strict line. Zack said, "For James to agree to organize our international conferences on genocide is worrisomely naive or, more worrisomely, misleading." It was said with so much venom that Ilka looked up, intercepting the look Zack and Yvette refrained from exchanging with each other. Ilka understood that they were—"in cahoots" was putting it too strongly—that they had talked the matter over, as they had every right to do, or, rather, that they had no need to talk to come out on the same side of this and every other question that was put before them. Ilka deduced some naked old grand-daddy of a skeleton.

A pause in which the members turned the pages of the candidate's vita. Those who had, for whatever reason, prejudged the matter on one side or the other wished to be observed being judicious, or prepared new ammunition. Those who didn't care one way or the other waited to see what they were going to think.

Alpha Stone said, "Perhaps the administrator should have clarified our requirements. The administrator goofed." Everybody smiled. The goofer was Alpha.

Zachariah said, "I asked James what he knew about computers, and he said, and I quote, 'Zilch.'"

"Which is par for the rest of us," said Alvin.

"Zack's point," Yvette said, "Is that we need someone who does know."

"So? The Computer Center people will come in and brief him."

Leslie said, "I see Zack's hand, I see Yvette, I see Alpha, I see Joe, whom I will take first because I've not heard from him yet." He wrote the names in order on a piece of paper, "Joe?"

Joe Bernstine had no axe of his own unless it was to help Leslie get what Leslie wanted. Leslie had his own reason—all things being equal—for wanting Ilka's young man hired. It would prevent himself from paying Ilka too much attention. Joe said, "How many of *us* have published four articles this year?"

"Yes, but where?" Yvette named a popular journal with the expression of one dangling a dead thing by its disagreeable tail.

"There are those among us," Alpha said, and refrained from exchanging a look with Alvin, and neither looked at Yvette, "who have published nothing at all."

A skeleton had put its foot in its mouth.

"He doesn't have a book," Zack said.

"He says it needs time to simmer."

"Since when do we hire people who don't have a book?"

"Since I was outvoted, on this very issue, in this very room, in the case of another candidate!" Everyone except Yvette knew Alpha meant Yvette.

"Ilka," Leslie said.

Ilka's number was to bring into the discussion what she believed to be the heart of every matter, and which, she knew, always seemed a given or an irrelevancy to everybody else: "Where is it written that everybody has to have a book?"

"Ilka, in our by-laws," Joe Bernstine said.

"Who made the by-laws?"

"The board of governors did, Ilka!"

"Who empowered the board of governors to make by-laws?"

"Leslie and I did, Ilka, fifteen years ago," Joe said.

"Aha! Who gave you and Leslie the power to empower the board?"

"Oy, Ilka!"

"No wait: Say my bell rings. Outside stands the policeman who might always be standing outside whenever a doorbell rings. The policeman has come to haul me to the police station, very appropriately—say that I have trashed the house I rent from the Rasmussens. Suppose I say, 'I'll go to the police station with you if you show me from whom you derive the power to haul me.'"

"They took it and everything else away from the Indians!" said Alvin.

"Wait! Who gave it to the Indians so it could be taken away from them?"

"Ilka!"

"Awooooooo," suddenly howled Nathan Cohn. He had been jotting things in the margins of Jimmy Carl's vita. He stood straight up and shouted, "What right do we think we have to pin down some poor sod's thoughts that he should be sleeping nights under his pillow wrestling with all the while we're chatting him up. I mean *what* in hell do we think we're we talking *about*!" and, the purple draining from his face, Nat sat down and wrote himself a note in the bottom margin.

Leslie asked if there was any more discussion. Everybody looked at everybody else. Everybody seemed tired. Leslie asked for a motion to vote, and the little blank papers were sent up each side of the table.

Jimmy Carl's move to Concordance coincided with the return of Ilka's landlords, the Rasmussens. Ilka had assumed she was going to buy a house but got frightened and rented from another couple on another sabbatical and Jimmy's things moved right in along with Ilka's. Ilka was not sorry. It was dear to wake with a male and human body asleep in her bed, on the window side, or not asleep after all. Submerged in this gorgeous commotion, Ilka forgot, for the moment, that other body—the one not available to her and which she had never nakedly so much as imagined—nor dared to want. Now she remembered how really fond she was of poor old actual Jimmy with his ribs and collarbone and too many elbows.

They were having a hilarious breakfast, deciding if the kitchen was the yellow of pure egg yolk or eggs scrambled, when Celie called from the office. Alpha had to catch the ten o'clock flight to New York. Could Jimmy make it to an eight-thirty meeting in Leslie's office? Jimmy might want to bring the list they'd asked him to prepare of prospective participants for the Genocide Conference.

"What list? Which conference is this?" Jimmy asked Ilka. "Where is Leslie's office?"

Ilka stayed in to get the house moved into. She called Jimmy midmorning. "Where, if you were the kind of person who had an egg-colored kitchen, would you be likely to keep your coffee filters?"

Jimmy said, "In the cupboard? Ilka, *I* don't know."

Ilka called ten minutes later. "They were in the drawer with the baby-bottle nipples, an expired card from the Forty-second Street library and negatives of somebody's wedding . . ."

"Ilka . . ." said Jimmy.

Ilka said, "Do you think you get insight into someone's soul by where they put things, where you would never think of putting them? Are there a sort of people who put all the jars—jam, honey, mustard, chutney—on the same shelf, and others who sort them according to sweet and savory?"

"I've got the computer man here."

"Oh! Sorry! I'll see you in the conference room at lunch."

"I'll see you, Ilka."

The computer man was a giant—Nordic, shoulders like Thor, hair like sunshine, welkin-eyed, nervous tic at the left corner of his mouth. He said, "This is your manuals."

Jimmy hefted them. He said, "I can't start on my conference list until I've got my desk cleared of all these directories and papers, memos, whatnot. Will the computer be able to make me a list of prospective participants according to their disciplines, with names, addresses, and credentials?"

The computer giant said, "You'll have to delimit the fields for your values, key in your codes, and enter your data."

"What's your name?" Jimmy asked the computer man.

"Sweng."

"I'm Jimmy. Sweng," Jimmy said, "can you translate from Turkish?"

"Turkish? No."

Jimmy said, "And I can't translate what you just said into what I am supposed to do." Jimmy sat down in the chair still warm from the computer giant's person and asked, "How do I enter?"

"You got to turn it on," said Sweng.

Jimmy was encouraged to see a switch that looked like other switches in his life. He turned it on and the screen engendered a lower case "b" that repeated itself to the rightmost margin, skipped left, filled the next line also and continued down the screen like this:

bbbbbbbbbbbbbbbbbbbbbbbbbbbbbbbbbbbbbbbbbbbbbbb
bbbbbbbbbbbbbbbbbbbbbbbbbbbbbbbbbbbbbbbbbbbbbbb
bbbbbbbbbbbbbbbbbbbbbbbbbbbbbbbbbbbbbbbbbbbbbbb
bbbbbbbbbbbbbbbbbbbbbbbbbbbbbbbbbbbbbbbbbbbbbbb
bbbbbbbbbbbbbbbbbbbbbbbbbbbbbbbbbbbbbbbbbbbbbbb
bbbbbbbbbbbbbbbbbbbbbbbbbbbbbbbbbbbbbbbbbbbbbbb
bbbbbbbbbbbbbbbbbbbbbbbbbbbbbbbbbbbbbbbbbbbbbbb
bbbbbbbbbbbbbbbbbbbbbbbbbbbbbbbbbbbbbbbbbbbbbbb
bbbbbbbbbbbbbbbbbbbbbbbbbbbbbbbbbbbbbbbbbbbbbbb
bbbbbbbbbbbbbbbbbbbbbbbbbbbbbbbbbbbbbbbbbbbbbbb
bbbbbbbbbbbbbbbbbbbbbbbbbbbbbbbbbbbbbbbbbbbbbbb
bbbbbbbbbbbbbbbbbbbbbbbbbbbbbbbbbbbbbbbbbbbbb . . .

"What did I do wrong?" cried Jimmy. "Did I ruin it?"

"Let me." Jimmy got gratefully out of the hot seat. Sweng sat down and punched a button. The witchery ceased.

"What did you do?" cried Jimmy. "Should I have known how to do that? *Now* what are you doing?" But answer came there none. The computer man punched buttons, gazed into the responding screen, punched and gazed. Useless for Jimmy to cry to him out of our common world, "I wish you would tell me what you're doing!" The computer man's soul had entered the computer. Jimmy watched and waited till the man rejoined himself, rose, and said, "You're O.K. now. Call the Computer Center if you have a question."

"Don't leave me!" cried Jimmy, but the computer giant ducked his head and cleared the door of Jimmy's office.

"I like it!" Jimmy reported to the conference table, where the institute people brought their democratic lunches. "I'm typing in lights! Words stay forever malleable, changeable like the words in my head! I love it when the screen produces a ghost line. You know how you know it's a ghost line?"

"It doesn't throw a shadow?" asked Alpha.

"It can't see itself in the mirror?" suggested Leslie.

"Little dogs bark at it?" proposed Ilka.

"Close! The little blinking cursor won't move along the ghost line; it moves only along the true line. That's sort of wonderful!"

Jimmy had mislaid his office, so Ilka walked him back. She laughed the third time they met on the stairs. It turned out that Jimmy was looking for the corridor that led to her office to ask her, "What's the name of what's his name's assistant?"

Martin Moses turned out to be whom Jimmy was looking for. "Which one is he?"

"Tall, funny. You talked with him for half an hour at the reception."

"I talked with a lot of funny people. Whose assistant did you say he is?"

"Zack's."

"Which one is Zack?"

"Nose in the middle of the face. Mouth like a keyhole."

"Ah. What does Zack do?"

"Jimmy, don't you have a listing of the members?"

"Probably underneath all the papers on my desk."

"Jimmy, there's a list—with your name newly penciled in—pinned on the cork board in the little lounge outside the kitchen."

"Which way is the kitchen?"

"Poor old Jimmy!" Eliza Shakespeare said to him. "It's hell to be new in a place and not know your way around, not know how it works." Eliza had dropped in shortly before five, and Leslie broke out a bottle of vodka. Someone got ice from the kitchen. Nobody felt like going home.

Ilka said, "My project is to not nag Jimmy."

They said, "That's right! You leave Jimmy alone!"

Ilka was surprised when, on their drive home, her mouth opened and said, "I was wondering, Jimmy, I mean, typing, is not exactly what you were hired to do, do you think?"

Jimmy said, "Not typing. Entering. I've got to get my desk cleared."

"I was only wondering," said Ilka and thought, wondering isn't nagging, "when you're going to get going on the conference?"

"When I've got my list entered in the computer."

Ilka thought she must surely be going to stop, however, she said, "I was only wondering when you'll finish getting it entered."

"Me too," Jimmy said. "That's just what I've been only wondering."

Ilka said nothing all the way up the narrow path to their front door. Poor Ilka! She came from a race of women who assumed that their men would drop things and fall over them, which the men generally went ahead and did. Ilka assumed that Jimmy was going to screw up and she minded for him. In the kitchen she ran herself a glass of water, swallowed it. Because of all Ilka did not say all the while they were undressing, she felt, when their paths crossed coming into, respectively out of, the bathroom, that she deserved a holiday from so much refraining and asked Jimmy, "When do you think you'll have enough essays for the book?"

"I'll let that simmer till I've got this conference under my belt."

From here on, all that Ilka refrained from saying to Jimmy freighted the air of the little borrowed house. It thickened the atmosphere in Jimmy's old Chevrolet, in which they rode to and from the institute together. Jimmy felt it whenever the air inside which he moved up and down the institute stairs or along the corridors briefly coincided with Ilka's air. Poor Jimmy!

———

A time passed. A Tuesday morning, and there was a memo from Alpha asking Jimmy to bring his list to the meeting at two. Jimmy turned the computer on, called the Computer Center, and asked, "How do I read my list?"

"What list is that?" asked the Computer Center.

Jimmy said, "My list of potential participants. I'm the new director of projects at the institute."

"Call up your SPAD Retrieval Screen."

"What's that?"

"Symbolic Program for Academic Disciplines."

Jimmy called back a few minutes later and said, "My manual doesn't have 'Retrieval.' The index skips from 'Reset all places,' to 'RFTCONV.EXE.' Please, are you a person with a name and a heart?"

"My name's Joel."

"Mine is Jimmy and I'm about to be a pain in your neck. Walk me through this retrieval maneuver, please."

"What are you looking for?"

"How about one crack international lawyer, one world class theologian, alternately ethicist, maybe a star doctor . . ."

"What's your value for law?" asked Joel.

"Comparatively high."

"What's your code?"

"Do you mean a number? On a scale from one to ten, say eight. Shall I enter eight?"

"What values do you want to run against it?"

Jimmy asked Joel if he knew Turkish. Joel was sorry but he had to meet his dad for lunch.

"You have a dad!" said Jimmy.

"You can say that again. Keep entering your values, punch Enter, enter the answer to the question on the Dialog Box, and punch Enter."

When the Dialog Box asked Jimmy "DWZ MSG 3714 A12 ?" he punched the Escape button. The screen replied, "FATAL ER-

ROR." Jimmy punched Escape again, and again the screen replied, "FATAL ERROR," and flashed off and on. Here's where Jimmy punched the Control button. The machine answered, "FATAL ERROR," and began to softly and mechanically roar. Jimmy punched Shift, he punched Caps Lock, he punched Scroll Lock, Control, Escape, Alt, Prtsc, Sys Req. The screen responded:

FATAL ERROR
FATAL ERROR
FATAL ERROR
FATAL ERROR
FATAL ERROR
FATAL ERROR

and flashed, and roared, and Jimmy let out a howl that brought Ilka, Celie, Barbara, Wendy, Alpha, Leslie Shakespeare, Zack, and Alvin running to his door.

"I'll reschedule for four," Leslie said to Jimmy. "Will that give you plenty of time?"

Joel did not get back from his lunch till quarter after three. "Did you enter your password?" he asked Jimmy.

"I have a password?"

"You have to make up a password," said Joel.

"I wish I were dead," said Jimmy.

"Can't have more than eight characters. Enter I-W-I-S-H-I-W-E, punch Enter. What does your screen say."

"ID, question mark?"

"Enter your ID . . . You don't have one? You have to request an ID from the security administration in writing."

Wendy passed Jimmy standing outside the door of the conference room. Jimmy said, "I'm breathing and waiting for my heart to slow down."

"Your heart is slowing down!" worried Wendy.

"As a matter of fact it's speeding up. Before it strangles my breathing altogether, here goes!" Jimmy opened the door and Alpha, Joe, Leslie, Nat, Ilka, Yvette, Zack, and Alvin turned and looked at him.

Jimmy said, "I didn't know there *was* a security administration. What all else might there be that I don't know!" Leslie looked at Jimmy with frank and, it seemed to Jimmy, appropriate, irritation. Jimmy looked affectionately at Leslie—a fine head! A beautiful man, and an honest one. Jimmy liked it that he was not able to seduce a smile out of Leslie.

Leslie said, "Bring in the old directories."

Jimmy said, "I haven't got the old directories."

"Where are they?"

"Lila put them away. I got Lila to clear my desk before she left to join her husband in Indo-China."

It turned out that the senior fellows had their own lists of prospects, and that Jimmy's job was to locate their present whereabouts and get off the letters of invitation.

"Use the directories in the University library," said Leslie.

Alpha said, "This is getting a bit late. People have schedules for the next year."

The directories through 1959 were bound in matte red, thereafter in dark blue that must have run out in '67, when the blue became fractionally grayer or was that a different directory? Jimmy took one of them down. It opened at page 1247. Jimmy went to the table where the librarian sat and asked her if it ever happened to her that she read a sentence that would not turn into meaning. The librarian was a little woman, not young, with a tender indoor pallor. Jimmy smiled into her eyes, but the librarian was not a smiler and hadn't the flirtatious instinct. She asked Jimmy what he was looking for. Jimmy followed her across the room saying,

"This is interesting: knowing how Washington works—who and where everybody is—or how, if you *don't* know, you can find out—makes me understand what all I don't know about the scholarly world." The librarian kept walking, Jimmy kept talking. "Do you remember being a little kid and knowing you didn't know what there was out there to know and not knowing what to ask?"

The librarian said, "Second and third shelves," and walked back to her chair behind the information desk. Jimmy took down "A–P," navy with self lettering. He was going to make it all the way to the "D's" without looking at the clock.

Jenny Bernstine called Ilka. "I met Jimmy at the library. Is he O.K.?"

"I don't think so," said Ilka. "He's living underwater and doesn't dare take the time to come up to breathe."

Weeks had passed. Alpha put her head in Jimmy's door and said, "Dyer says he hasn't got our letter."

"It's in the batch I got off yesterday," lied Jimmy. His scalp prickled.

"Oh, good!" Alpha said, "Do remember, Jimmy, to always put copies of all outgoing correspondence in the ring folder in the lounge, so every member can keep track of what everyone is doing."

"I'll run it right out." Jimmy waited for her to close the door behind her. Using both his hands for shovels, he churned the new agglomeration of papers on his desk.

Alpha phoned from her office to say, "I called Paul back to say the letter's in the mail, but he's leaving the end of this week. Better send a duplicate to him in Oxford."

"Will do," said Jimmy. Jimmy called Joel. "Sorry but come over and help me, please. Now!"

Jimmy assumed eyes behind the horn-rims, a mouth inside the beard, feet—sockless—inside the frayed tennis shoes. "I need the address of a man name of Dyer, and I don't know how to call my list up!"

Joel sat in Jimmy's chair, punched, gazed, and asked, "Did you Control KD it? Looks like the job abended."

"Abended is what?"

"DB zapped."

"What does it mean? I mean so what do I have on the computer?"

"You don't," Joel said and he returned to his Computer Center.

"What are you doing on the floor?" Ilka stood in the doorway.

"Putting my papers in order," said Jimmy. He had pulled the bottom drawer all the way out, upturned it on the carpet, and was aligning papers and envelopes according to their size and kind. "I can't find Dyer's address. Maybe it's D-*I*-E-R."

"How likely are you to find it in the drawer in which you keep your blank institute stationery?"

"So unlikely that when I fail to find it I won't jump out of the window."

"Why don't you ask Alpha!"

"*NO!*" shouted Jimmy. "I can't."

"Why, Jimmy, can't you ask Alpha for an address?"

Jimmy put his head into his hands and said, "Did you know panic can be located? The prickling is on the *inside* of the scalp; there's a grinding sort of roiling and it's right under the ribs in the place you'd expect to feel hunger. And there is a simultaneous silent roaring not, interestingly, in the ears."

"Jimmy, you want *me* to go ask Alpha?"

"NO!!!" shouted Jimmy and he leaned his cheek against Ilka and put his arms around her shoulders like a pugilist hanging his weight round his adversary's neck for a moment's breather. He said, "I earnestly wish that I were dead." Ilka, stroking his hair, aborted her answering thought.

Jimmy said, "Marry me, Ilka!"

Ilka said, "All right," and waited for something friendly that she must surely, on the occasion, be going to say to Jimmy.

"So. I guess Jimmy and I are going to be married."

"We'll make you a reception," said Eliza. "Our gooseberries are ripe! Do you and Jimmy like gooseberries?" She reached for the cookbook on the shelf behind her.

If Eliza had asked Ilka, "And are you happy?" Ilka would have said, "Sure. I kind of love Jimmy," but Eliza said, "Gooseberry, gooseberry, gooseberry. Here: Gooseberry. Gooseberry jelly; Gooseberry pudding, baked; Pudding, boiled! Chhhh! Gooseberry sauce for boiled mackerel? Hm. Gooseberry tart, trifle . . ."

Ilka said, "You don't know what it's like waking every morning wishing the person in your bed, whom you are really fond of, weren't really there."

"Not every morning," said Eliza.

"I don't believe you!" cried Ilka. "You can't wish Leslie weren't there! Eliza, Jimmy is not going to hack it, and he knows it, and he's frightened. Leslie does everything he does right!"

"That's right," said Eliza. "You don't wake up every morning next to somebody who does everything right. You think Leslie and I don't look across the bed and wish each other dead?"

"Yes. I think you don't."

"Here: Gooseberry fool!" said Eliza. "Green gooseberries: to every pint of pulp add one pint of milk or a half pint of cream and sugar to taste. Leslie loves gooseberry fool."

The fool was a delicious fool, and Leslie made a ceremony of the superb champagne. They sat where of all places Ilka most loved to sit—in the Shakespeares' living room. Ilka's mother had

come from New York, and there were the Bernstines and the
Stones, the Cohns, Zachariah and Maria, Alvin and Alicia, and
Yvette Gordot. Why was Ilka surprised that they had got to love
Jimmy?

"We'll buy a house," said Ilka.

Jimmy said, "Wait till my retention meeting. What if I get
fired?"

Ilka started looking for her house.

Alpha called Jimmy's office and said, "It's a jinx. Paul thinks it's
the English postal service."

"I'll get out a duplicate of the duplicate."

Jimmy sat in Eliza Shakespeare's kitchen. She filled his glass
with white table wine, and he said "Thanks!" Eliza filled her own
glass. Jimmy watched Eliza move from the sink to the icebox to
the stove. He said, "Ilka has made a lap, and bent her head over it.
Her arms bend forward at shoulder level, and again at the elbows,
and the wrists—a three-hundred-and-sixty-degree embrace, an
egg-shape. An egg turns a single shoulder to everything on the
outside—including me! Thanks." Eliza had refilled his glass.
"Shouldn't the father be an insider? She doesn't even nag me any
more!"

Eliza set a plate in front of Jimmy and watched him taste.
"This is unbelievable. Aren't you going to eat?"

"Maybe not just yet." Eliza helped him to salad and refilled his
glass, and her own. She lit herself a cigarette. Jimmy said, "You
know what ambrosia is really? It's what tastes like the smell
promises. Imagine coffee tasting like the smell of fresh ground
beans; fresh ground pepper, bananas. This is that sort of a taste!"
Eliza refilled their glasses. Jimmy said, "You know what writing
my book feels like? Like having got up from a very large, very rich
and greasy meal and having to make yourself sit down to eat a very
large, rich, greasy meal: it's what of all things in all the world,

you most want to not do. Does Leslie tell you all my fuckups?"
Jimmy told Eliza about aligning the blank institute stationary:
"If I create this Platonic order, mustn't everything, by definition,
be where it ought to be, and wouldn't I find the letter I ought to
have written to an Englishman called Dyer or maybe D I E R? Or
D I N E R? D R I E R? D R I N E R?"

Eliza said, "Let's creep upstairs and poke around Leslie's
desk!"

"You want Paul B. *Thayer*," said Eliza. "Old Oxford buddy of
Leslie's. Theologian at Brasenose!"

Jimmy sobbed and put his arms around Eliza and kissed her
and she kissed him. All the way down the stairs she kept picking
his hands like so many burrs off her nape, her hip, her breast but
let him keep his head on her shoulder and finish sobbing before
she got him inched out the door.

Jimmy was not going to the Summer Fiesta with Ilka and the
Shakespeares. Jimmy was going to the office to get some letters
written—get on top of things.

The Concordance Institute on a Sunday put Jimmy in mind of
the lush melancholy of August in Manhattan when one's friends
have gone away. All afternoon Jimmy thought he could hear,
over the sound of paper against paper, a distant music, squalls of
laughter. By the time he had his briefcase filled with the work he
could do at home, the day had come to the long blue moment for
which Nat Cohn was still seeking the exact adjective. Ilka might
be home by now. Damned if he was going to walk all the way by
the Northgate. He could cross South Meadow, cut through the
project and come out a block from home before it got really dark.

Jimmy stepped out the front door, locked it and walked round
to the back where tree, bush, and grass already shaded toward
night. It intensified the yellow of the tea roses, developed the
blue component of the reds to purple; the whites had become

transparent, ghostly. Overgrown sprigs reached for Jimmy's trouser legs, barbed branches grabbed his hair like the shoots that grew into the hundred-year-high wall of thorns in which Sleeping Beauty's would-be lovers starved to death, dozens—hundreds— of beautiful young princes though some might have got stuck because they were too stout, or inclined to tell jokes that never worked out, or too shy to get the conversation going.

The garden gate needed oiling. Jimmy walked out onto the playing field. People were still about. He walked watching them play the old game of two against the middle. He couldn't tell, at this distance, what the thing was the one on the left tossed to the one on the right, over the head and just out of reach of the middle one, who leaped and leaped and presently caught and put it on his head—a baseball cap. He ran with it toward the right thrower who was running to meet him. Jimmy watched the two approach each other over the darkening expanse. Jimmy never mentioned, even to Ilka, that watching the two put their heads together he had experienced the same deep charm he felt before the Metropolitan Museum's iron-age sculpture of what's hardly more than a stick figure resting a hand on the shoulder of just such another. The descriptive tablet says they're battling, but Jimmy understood it as a gesture of affectionate friendship, of one saying something the other understood. The figures on the meadow parted. The other thing Jimmy was going to be embarrassed to remember was his elation at the elegant choreography of their running side-by-side toward him. At a point, still running, they parted, approaching him in a pincer movement, and Jimmy understood he was about to be mugged. The boy on the left hurled himself against Jimmy, knocking him onto his right knee at the precision moment in which the one on his right, who turned out to be a girl, yanked his briefcase with a clean jerk from underneath his arm. Jimmy turned and watched them running, side-by-side, bearing away the briefcase with the letter to Paul Thayer that Jimmy had forgotten to drop into the institute mail chute.

Jimmy and Ilka moved into their new house in September and Maggie was born the first of November. "We're never more than half awake. It's a luxurious sort of underwater motion."

"I remember," Eliza said. "I remember."

"Why am I standing in the hallway? Ah! That's the baby crying. I go in. I pick up the baby. It's 2 A.M. and the lights are on downstairs in poor Jimmy's study. We've asked my mother to come and help."

Ilka's mother came. Now when Ilka went in to check the baby her mother Flora was always already there, whether it was two in the afternoon or night. Ilka's mother fed the baby and bathed the baby. She pushed Ilka out of the way with her elbow and would have taken Maggie out of the pediatrician's arms if the doctor hadn't pushed Ilka's mother out of the way to put the baby into Ilka's arms. Ilka, who liked her mother better than she liked the doctor, was sorry for Flora, who was embarrassed and said, "I mean I thought because Ilka is wearing her brooch..." Ilka's mother was stunned when Ilka and Jimmy eventually suggested she might want to go back to New York. "We'll come and visit for the winter holiday," promised Ilka.

The institute needed Jimmy to drive to Washington. Leslie called Ilka and said, "Might it be a good idea to have him out of town while we meet about his retention?" Ilka thought that it was a good idea.

Leslie said, "I've accepted Ilka's request to disqualify herself. I see Zack's hand. I see Alvin's hand, I see Yvette, in that order."

Zack said, "Is it the sense of this committee that Jimmy is organizing this conference?"

Alvin said, "Well, he's had his way to find around the institute."

"And lost our directories," Yvette said.

"Is it the sense of this committee that Jimmy is writing a book?"

"It's still simmering," Yvette said.

"Because he's had a conference to organize," Alvin said.

"He's had a baby," Joe said.

"It's not a baby, it's a book he contracted to have."

"Don't we know we ask our young people to commit themselves to what is impossible to accomplish."

"And to which they contractually commit themselves."

"And which every one of us around this table has at one time or another accomplished."

"And never in the time specified. How can we fire poor Jimmy after wasting two years out of his life . . ." Alvin stopped. Everyone's ears pricked up at a tiny but distinct sound like a vase breaking in a distant room.

Zack said, "Amazing! We say, 'Let's give this incompetent time to prove himself.' The incompetent proves himself to be incompetent and we worry about wasting his time! While Jimmy's chums congratulate themselves on the milk of their human kindness, they might ask themselves if it mightn't be humane to relieve the young man of the awful experience of not being capable . . ." Zack, too, stopped. The members of the committee who sat with their backs to the window saw the white wall blush, saw the members across the table raise their eyes to the window, and looked around and saw the sky flare with a sudden wartime redness that went as suddenly out.

"Interesting," said Joe, "that we leave out of the equation how very well Jimmy writes. Don't we know that writing takes as long as it takes? Is there anyone around this table who didn't know the time Jimmy projected for the completion of his book bore no relation to the time it might actually take him, but was predicated on the time we required him to say that he was going to take, in order to give him a job?"

"He agreed contractually," said Zack.

Here's where Nat Cohn turned purple, got up, shouted, and sat down.

Leslie said. "I see Alpha, then Yvette . . ." It wasn't until Leslie passed the blank papers up both sides of the table that there was a knock on the door. Leslie frowned at Wendy, "We're in committee, I told you . . ." Wendy kept standing in the doorway. Leslie said, "Would you all excuse me," and went outside.

When the bell rang Ilka put the baby into the crib and went down the stairs. Outside the door stood two policemen. The baby, Ilka thought, remembered she had set the baby down in the crib in her room at the top of the stairs, and said, "My mother!" subliminally wondering how the Concordance police could have jurisdiction over a calamity that would have to have happened in New York. The little Spanish policeman was Juan Jose who had come with Officer Right when the institute copier went missing. His upper lip had always looked naked to Ilka as if it must once have had, or ought to have, a mustache. And the other policeman was too young—a big, boy policeman who looked underdone as if he had raw sex on his mind. Ilka said, "My husband?" Officer Jose asked if they could come inside. It took a time for him to step far enough into the hall for the big boy policeman to be able to get far enough in to get the door closed behind them. The two policemen filled the little hallway. They looked gently at Ilka, which frightened her. "It's my husband!" They did not deny it. Officer Jose said the car made an explosion and seemed to be pointing in a southerly direction. Ilka said, "It made what?"

If she had understood what was intended by the edge of the

seat of the chair chafing the back of her knees Ilka would have been glad to sit down. "Lady," the little Officer Jose kept saying, "Miss! Lady! You make yourself sick, lady." Ilka sympathized with the two policemen's not wishing to be in the same room with her noise and would willingly have undertaken to stop screaming if she had been at leisure: Ilka had latched onto the notion of a mistake. Disasters in a Spanish accent did not have to be real. Ilka stopped screaming and asked for the number.

"Lady? What number?"

"The number, the number," Ilka said irritably, "of security."

The Spanish policeman told Ilka a number. He wrote the number on the back of the paper that had Ilka's name and address on it. Ilka dialed and said, "This is Ilka Carl," and gave her address and said: "Would you please send a . . ." and stopped. She had been going to say 'send a real policeman,' meaning a weighty, elderly white policeman. "Sorry!" she said to the small Spanish policeman, and hung up, and said again, "I'm sorry," however she continued for the rest of the evening to wait for the bell to ring and Officer Right to come in and Jimmy's car to not have exploded. Now Ilka remembered the baby in her crib at the top of the stairs, who must have heard the screaming. Ilka said, "Excuse me," to the two policemen and ran up the stairs.

The baby, Maggie, had lately learned how to sit, but not, once she sat, to lie down. Her enormous eyes stared between the slats of the crib. Ilka took the little girl up and wrapped her in her arms, and that was when Ilka swallowed. What Ilka swallowed was the fact that Jimmy was dead and she said, "Poor daddy's car is broken. Come and say hello to the policemen," in the normal voice that would henceforward emanate so curiously out of her throat and mouth, and then the doorbell rang. Ilka met the boy policeman galumphing up the stairs.

"Miss, where do you want we should put it?"

"Put it?" asked Ilka.

"Put him," said the policeman.

"Ah. Where do you think?"

The boy policeman waited for Ilka to do the thinking. "Put him . . . put him in the big bedroom?"

Ilka hid in the kitchen with the baby, chattering about juice and the whereabouts of the pretty blue bottle and whatever the matter could be with the silly nipple that would not and would not go on the silly bottle, but the baby kept turning her head around and her gaze fixed in the direction of the closed door on the other side of which the two male voices were trying to figure a method by which the stretcher might be maneuvered in the front door and angled up the narrow stair. Ilka went to the kitchen door to say, "Maybe just put him in the study downstairs," but the stretcher was stuck on the banister. Officer Jose, who was backing up the steps, must be at the head end. He said, "Move, lady, please," and to the boy at what had to be Jimmy's feet, he said, "*Left!* You go left, and lift, I told you. Move back. *Back* and *lift!* Higher."

Ilka returned to the kitchen and fed the baby, and presently she heard the men's footsteps coming down the stairs. When Ilka went to carry the baby up, the two policeman stood by the hall mirror and turned their startled, apologetic faces as if Ilka had caught them out. Ilka understood that they were not going to go away. "You can sit in the living room," she said to them, but when she came down they were huddling in the kitchen. "It's all right," she told them, but they scuttled out into the hallway and huddled in the curl of the banister. Ilka asked them if they would like a cup of coffee, but they shook their heads vigorously, in unison. Later Ilka happened upon the big boy policeman peeing in the bathroom. He said, "Oops," and she said, "Sorry." When the doorbell began to ring, the young policeman detailed himself to let people in. Joe and Jenny Bernstine came first with horrified faces. The young policeman opened the door to the Shakespeares. Eliza was weeping. Ilka moved into the other woman's arms. Leslie asked Ilka if she would like him to make arrangements.

"Arrangements. Yes. Please! He's upstairs on the bed."

"Who is upstairs?"

"Jimmy. In the big bedroom."

"What do you mean? In this house? They *brought him into the house!* Christ!" Leslie's mouth made a thin, ferocious line. Not an attractive line. "Ilka, go answer the door. Let me deal with this."

The Stones had arrived, and Alvin and Alicia, and Zack and Maria. Ilka saw Leslie talking to the little Spanish policeman. Ilka saw Leslie sitting at the phone on the console in the hall and said, "Leslie. Thank you." Leslie rapidly dipped and shook his head, rose, took Ilka's hand and kissed it. "I'm going to see the coroner. If you give me addresses, I'll call his family."

Ilka knew Leslie had left the house. Nancy Cohn stood in the window crying bitterly. There was food on trays and in baskets. "Thanks," Ilka said. "Where is the baby?"

"Bethy has taken her to play out in the yard, O.K.?"

Ilka kept saying "thanks" to people. "Does anybody want some coffee?" she asked them.

Everybody said, "No thanks."

Leslie said, "I would very much like some coffee." Leslie had returned? Ilka was in the kitchen filling a kettle with water, measuring coffee, when Officer Jose came and stood in the kitchen door. He asked Ilka if she minded if he studied his book for this exam a week from Tuesday, to make sergeant. Ilka took him into Jimmy's study and cleared Jimmy's papers onto a chair. Ilka walked upstairs. She went into the bedroom. That was Jimmy under the white sheet. Ilka didn't recognize the sheet—it was not one of her sheets. Would Ilka have turned the sheet back if the very large, embarrassed boy policeman hadn't stood in the door and asked if she minded if he watched the playoffs, his favorite team? His brother's best friend was a rookie fullback. Ilka minded very much, but couldn't think if that was right or not. She couldn't figure out why Jimmy's being dead under the alien sheet should prevent a bored boy from watching his brother's best friend on his favorite team. She said, "Get yourself a chair out of the baby's room at the top of the stairs," but the policeman said, "That's O.K." Ilka understood that he wanted to be a minimum of bother. She understood that her presence prevented him from turning the TV on, so she went out of the room. The TV stood on the dresser. It troubled Ilka that the boy would have to sit on the edge of the bed to watch. Would he budge Jimmy's legs under that sheet to make room? As long as Ilka lived she wondered about not having turned the sheet back to look at Jimmy when he was dead. And she tried imagining a way for the young policeman to have sat on the edge of the bed without having to move Jimmy's legs.

It wasn't till evening that the coroner's men came with a folded stretcher. Leslie walked outside and closed the door and talked with them and came back in and said, "Ilka, take the baby into the living room."

"No!" shouted Ilka. "I want to stand here!" Ilka stood at the bottom of the stairs. She shivered and someone put a sweater around her shoulders. "Thank you," she said. The phone rang. Someone handed Ilka the receiver. Ilka's friend, Carter, was calling. "Just happened to be thinking about you," he said, "wondering how you're doing."

Ilka said, "Jimmy died."

"We have a bad connection," said Carter on the other side of the continent. "I don't understand what you are saying."

"Yes, you do," Ilka said, "Jimmy is dead. They're bringing him down the stairs."

"Christ!" Carter said. "This is embarrassing."

"No, it's not! It's not embarrassing! Why is being dead embar-rassing!" howled Ilka as the two men lifted Jimmy over the ban-ister. They got him angled out the door, carried him down the path and out of the gate. They put him in the back of the coro-ner's truck and drove away.

OTHER PEOPLE'S
DEATHS

Everybody Leaving

The coroner's men put James in the back of the truck and drove away, and the Bernstines, once again, urged Ilka to come home with them, at least for the night, or let them take the baby. Again Ilka was earnest in begging to be left right here, wanted the baby to stay here with her. No thank you, really, she did not need—did not want—anybody sleeping over.

The friends and colleagues trooped down the path, the Shakespeares, the Bernstines, the Ayes, the Zees, the Cohns, and the Stones. Outside the gate they stopped, they looked back, but Ilka had taken the baby inside and closed the door. They stood a moment, they talked, not accounting to themselves for the intense charm of the summer hill rising behind Ilka's house, of standing, of breathing—of the glamour of being alive. Leslie asked everyone to come over for a drink.

They moved along the sidewalk in groups and pairs. Dr. Alfred Stone walked with his wife. The report of the accident had come in the very the moment the committee was about to vote on Jimmy's retention. Alpha had called Alfred. It was he who attended at the scene. Dr. Stone was arranging the sentence he ought to have spoken to the widow when he arrived at her house or at some moment in the hours since. Everybody stopped at the corner. Ilka's door was open. The two policemen who had spent the day trying to be inconspicuous were finally able, now that the body had been removed, to go home. The smaller, Spanish policeman walked out the gate, but the big young policeman turned and waved. Ilka must be standing back in the darkness. The two policemen got into the police car and drove away.

Inside her foyer Ilka closed the door and leaned her head against it, devastated at everybody's leaving.

Words to Speak to the Widow

At the Shakespeares' there was the business of walking into the sitting room, of sitting down, of the drinks. "A lot of ice, Leslie. Thanks." "Martini, please, and hold the vegetables."

Joe Bernstine smiled sadly. "I wonder if we retained Jimmy."

Leslie said, "Alpha will schedule us a new search committee."

Nobody said, We could hardly do worse than poor Jimmy.

Jenny Bernstine said, "Ilka is being very gallant and terrific."

Nobody said, She didn't cry.

Alicia said, "Ilka isn't one to throw her hands up."

"Or the towel in, *or* the sponge," said Eliza. "Joke. Sorry."

Alicia said, "Ilka is not one to drown in her sorrows."

"Well I'm going to drown mine," Eliza held her glass out to Leslie, who refilled it.

Alicia said, "We live on borrowed time."

Alpha asked her husband, "The policeman said there was fire?" and the friends' and colleagues' imaginations went into action to dim or scramble or in some way unthink the flames in which Jimmy—the person they knew—was burning. They wanted not to have an image of which they would never after be able to rid themselves.

Dr. Stone replied that there was fire but Jimmy's body had been thrown clear. The fall had broken his neck.

The flames were gone. The friends envisaged the unnaturally angled head with Jimmy's face.

Dr. Alfred Stone took his drink. He sat down. He looked around the room and located his wife sitting beside Eliza Shakespeare. Were they talking about the death? Alfred had, earlier in the day, seen Alpha talking with Ilka and had wondered what words Alpha might be saying to the widow: To refer to the death would be like putting a finger in a wound, but how *not* mention it? And wasn't it gross to be talking of anything else? Alfred mistakenly believed himself to be singularly lacking in what normal people—the people in this room—were born knowing. He thought all of them knew how to feel and what to say. He watched them walk out and return with drinks. They stood together and talked. Dr. Stone remained sitting.

At eleven o'clock that first night, as a brutal loneliness knocked the wind out of Ilka, her phone rang. "We thought we'd see how you were doing," said Leslie. "Did the baby get to sleep?"

"The baby is O.K. I'm O.K. Is it O.K. to be O.K.? I could do with some retroactive lead time. I need to practice taking my stockings off with Jimmy dead. Relearn how to clean my teeth."

Leslie said, "Wait." Ilka heard him pass on to Eliza, who must be in the room, who might be lying in the bed beside him, that Ilka was O.K. but needed to relearn how to clean her teeth with

Jimmy dead. His voice returned full strength. "Eliza says we're coming over in the morning to bring you breakfast."

Sitting Shiva

"I don't know how," said Ilka. Joe Bernstine remembered that when his father died, his mother had turned the faces of the mirrors to the wall. Ilka was struck with the gesture but embarrassed by its drama. "I know I'm supposed to sit on a low stool, but I can't get any lower." Ilka was sitting on the floor tickling Maggie, the fat, solemn, comfortable baby. Baby Maggie's eyes were so large they seemed to go around the corner of the little face with its baroque hanging cheeks.

"A Viennese baby," Eliza said.

"She's fun to hold because she collapses her weight in your arms." Ilka jumped Maggie up and down. "She must have heard me scream when the policemen told me."

Eliza unpacked the tiny tomatoes from her garden. She had baked two long loaves of white bread. Jenny was arranging the cold cuts that she had brought onto the platters she had also brought. At some point in the morning Joe and Leslie rose to go to the institute. They would be back in an hour. Leslie took Ilka's hand and brought it to his lips.

Ilka said, "I called my mother and she is coming tomorrow."

In the Institute

Celie at her desk across from the front entrance fanned herself with an envelope like one trying to avoid fainting. She told Betty, "I talked with him that actual morning! He comes running in, punches the elevator button, doesn't wait and runs right up those stairs, comes right down. He's stuffing papers in his briefcase. I told him, 'You have a good trip now,' and he says, 'Oh shit!' and he's going to run back up except the elevator door opens, and he gets in, and goes back up."

Betty was able to one-up Celie with her spatial proximity to the dead man, though at a greater temporal remove. The day *before* James drove to Washington he tried to open the door into the conference room with papers under his arm, carrying a cup of coffee, saying, "Anybody got a spare hand?" Betty had held the door for him. He had said "Oh! Thanks!"

Could a person for whom one held a door, who said "Oh shit!" and "Oh! Thanks!" be dead?

Words to Write to the Widow

Nancy Cohn and Maria Zee talked on the telephone and one-upped each other in respect to which of them was the more upset. "I got to my office," said Maria, "and just sat."

"I," Nancy said, "never made it to the office because I'd kept waking up every hour *on* the hour."

"I never got to sleep! I kept waking poor Zack to check if he was alive. He was furious."

"Have you called her?"

"I thought I would write."

"That's what I'll do. I'll write her," said Nancy.

Sitting Shiva, Day Two

"It's good of you to come," Ilka said to the visitors. The institute staff, Celie, Betty, Wendy, and Barbara dropped over together, after office hours. They sat round the table in Ilka's kitchen. The fellows sat in the living room. Ilka's mother held the baby on her lap. Ilka let out a sudden laugh. "What'll I do when the party is over!" She rose and took the baby and carried her out of the room past Dr. Stone hiding in the foyer.

Dr. Stone believed that by the time Ilka returned he would be ready with the right sentence, but when she came down Alfred was glad that the baby's head intervened between his face and Ilka's face so that it was not possible to say anything to her and the front-door bell was ringing again. Martin Moses walked in, took Ilka and her baby into a big hug, and said, "Christ, Ilka!" Ilka said, "Don't I know it."

"Give her to me," Ilka's mother said and took the child out of Ilka's arms.

Alpha came out of the living room saying, "Hello, Martin. Ilka, listen, take it easy. You take a couple of days—as long as you like, you know that! Alfred, we have to go." And the Ayes and the Zees had to go home. Celie and the rest left. Martin left. The Shakespeares said they would be back. Ilka thought everyone had gone when she heard the gentle clatter in the kitchen. Jenny Bernstine was washing dishes.

People trickled over in the evening—a smaller crowd that left sooner. Jenny washed more dishes. When Joe came to pick her up, she looked anxiously at Ilka, who said, "I'm O.K."

Writing to the Widow

Nancy Cohn went to look for Nat. He was on the living-room couch watching TV.

Nancy said, "I'm embarrassed not to know what to write to Ilka. It's embarrassing worrying about being embarrassed for Chrissake!"

"Calamity is a foreign country. We don't know how to talk to the people who live there."

Nancy said, "*You* write her. You're the writer in the family."

"I'm not feeling well," said Nat.

"She's *your* colleague!" said Nancy.

And so neither of them wrote to Ilka.

Maria called Alicia and asked her, "I mean, we went *over* there. Do we still have to write?"

Alicia said, "Alvin says we'll have her over next time we have people in."

A Casserole

Celie cooked a casserole and told Art, her thirteen-year-old, to take it over to Mrs. Carl's house.

"The woman that her husband burned up in his car? No way!"

Linda, who was fifteen, said, "For your information, he did *not* even burn up. He broke his neck." She advised her brother to check his facts.

Art said, "Linda will go and take it over to her."

Well, Linda wasn't going over there, not by herself, so Celie made them both go.

Nobody answered the front bell.

Art said, "I never knew a dead person before."

Linda said, "You mean you never knew a person, and afterwards they died and you didn't as a *fact* even know this person at all."

Art said, "But I know mom, and mom knew him. Ring it again."

They found a couple of bricks, piled one on top of the other and took turns standing on them to look in the window. Those were the stairs the dead man must have walked up and down on. There was a little table with a telephone on it and a chair. Had the dead man sat on that exact chair and lifted that phone to his ear?

Running Away

Yvette, who had not called on Ilka, drove over, rang the bell, saw the casserole by the front door, thought, She's out, skipped down the steps, got in her car, and drove away.

"Ilka was out, with the baby," Dr. Alfred Stone reported to his wife, "and I practically fell over the stroller, corner of Euclid."

"What did you say to her?" Alpha asked him

"Say?" said Alfred. "Nothing. She was across the street on the other sidewalk."

Trying to imagine an impossibility hurts the head. Having failed to envisage Alfred falling over a stroller that was on the other sidewalk, Alpha chose to assume that she had missed or misunderstood some part of what he had told her.

Alfred came to remember not what had happened but what he said had happened. The unspoken words he owed the widow displaced themselves into his chest and gave him heartburn.

Night Conversation

"Celie left a casserole. Alfred fell into Maggie's stroller," Ilka reported to the Shakespeares, when they called that night.

Leslie said, "Eliza says, What did Alfred say?"

"He slapped his forehead the way you're supposed to slap your forehead when you remember something you've forgotten—and ran across the street to the other sidewalk. Poor Alfred! He's so beautiful."

Eliza took the phone from Leslie. "Why 'poor Alfred' when he's behaving like a heel?"

Ilka said, "Because Jimmy's death is making him shy of me. He thinks it's impolite of him to be standing upright."

Eliza said, "The good lord intended Alfred to be your basic shit, and Alfred went into medicine in the hope of turning into a human being."

"Doesn't he get points for hoping?"

"Why can't you just be offended?"

"Don't know," said Ilka again. "I mean people can't help being shits."

"You sound like Jimmy," said Eliza. Ilka listened and heard the sound, over the telephone, of Eliza weeping for Ilka's husband.

Inviting the Widow

Nancy said, "We'll have her in when we have people over. The Stones are coming Sunday. Only, you think she wants to be around people?"

"Call her and ask her," said Nat.

"You call her and ask her."

"*I'm* not going to call her. You call her."

"She's *your* colleague, *you* call her."

"I'm not well."

"I don't think she wants to be around people," Nancy said. "And her mother is staying with her."

Dr. Alfred Stone

Dr. Alfred Stone continued to mean to say to the widow what, as a doctor—as the doctor who had been on the scene of the accident—he ought and must surely be going to say to her. He always thought that by the next time he was face to face with her he was going to have found the appropriate words and blushed crimson when he walked into the Shakespeares' kitchen and saw little

Maggie sitting on a high chair and Ilka crawling underneath the table. She said, "Hi, Alfred. Look what Maggie did to poor Eliza's floor. And now Bethy is going to take Maggie to play in the yard so the grown-ups can sit down in peace and quiet. O.K., Bethy. She's all yours."

Bethy had grown bigger and bulkier. The bend of Bethy's waist, as she buttoned the baby into her sweater, cried out to her parents, to her parents' friends: Watch me buttoning the baby's sweater! Bethy's foot on the back stair into the yard pleaded, This is me taking the baby into the yard. Notice me!

Murphy's Law seated Dr. Alfred Stone next to the widow. While the conversation was general, he tried for a sideways view of her face which was turned to Eliza on her other side. Alfred was looking for the mark on Ilka, the sign that her husband had been thrown from a burning car and had broken his neck. Alfred studied his wife across the table. Would Alpha, if he, Alfred, broke *his* neck, look so regular and ordinary? Would she laugh at something Eliza said?

As they were leaving, Alpha asked Ilka to dinner and Ilka said, "If I can get a sitter. My mother has gone back to New York." Jenny Bernstine offered Bethy.

After that and for the next weeks, the friends and colleagues invited Ilka to their dinners. She always said yes. "I'm afraid," she told the Shakespeares, "that my first No, thank you, will facilitate the next no and start a future of noes." Then, one day, as she was driving herself to the Zees', Ilka drove past their house, made a U-turn, and drove home. She insisted on paying Bethy for the full evening.

"We missed you," Leslie said on the telephone.

"How come it gets harder instead of easier? You put on your right stocking and there's the left stocking to still be put on, and the right and left shoe . . ." Ilka heard Leslie tell Eliza what Ilka said.

In the morning, Ilka called Maria to apologize and Maria said, "Don't be silly!"

"A rain check?"

"Absolutely," said Maria. "Or you call me."

"Absolutely," said Ilka. But Ilka did not call her, and Maria did not call Ilka. One's house seemed more comfortable without Ilka from Calamity.

Bethy Bernstine

The Bernstines and the Shakespeares were the true friends. Ilka loved them and missed Jimmy because he was missing Eliza's beautiful risotto and Leslie's wine that yielded taste upon taste on the tongue. Ilka held out her glass, watched Joe's hand tip the bottle and thought, Joe will die, not now, not soon, but he will die. Ilka saw Jenny looking at her with her soft, anxious affection and thought, Jenny will die. "Will you forgive me," Ilka said to them, "if I take myself home?" Of course, of course! Leslie must drive Ilka. "Absolutely not! Honestly! You would do me the greatest possible favor if you would let me go by myself." "Joe will drive Ilka." "Let me drive you!" said Joe. "No, no, no!" cried Ilka. They could see that she was distraught. "Let Ilka alone," said Leslie. "Ilka will drive herself. Ilka will be fine."

Leslie and Joe came out to put Ilka into her car. She saw them, in her rearview mirror as she drove away, two old friends standing together, talking on the sidewalk. There would be a time when both of them would have been dead for years.

Bethy was curled on the couch, warm and smelling of sleep, her skin sweet and dewy. Cruel for a sixteen-year-old to be plain—too much chin and jowl, the little, pursed, unhappy mouth. Ilka woke

Bethy with a hand on her shoulder. She helped the young girl collect herself, straighten her bones, pick her books off the floor. Ilka walked her out and stood on the sidewalk.

Maggie was sleeping on her back, arms above her head, palms curled. In her throat, and behind her eyes, Ilka felt the tears she could not begin to cry. Ilka feared that beast in the jungle which might, some day, stop the tears from stopping.

When Leslie called to make sure she had got home, Ilka said, "I've been doing arithmetic. Subtract the age I am from the age at which I'm likely to die and it seems like a hell of a lot of years."

Though the words Dr. Alfred Stone had failed to say to Ilka had become inappropriate and could never be said, he tended, when they were in the same room, to move along the wall at the furthest remove from where Ilka might be moving or standing or sitting.

The Howling

REVERSE BUG

"Let's get the announcements out of the way," said Ilka to her students in Conversational English. "Tomorrow evening the institute is holding a symposium. Ahmed," she asked the Turkish student with the magnificently drooping mustache, "where are they holding the symposium?"

"In the New Theater," said Ahmed.

"The theme," said the teacher, "is 'Should there be a statute of limitations on genocide?' with a wine and cheese reception . . ."

". . . In the lounge . . . ," said Ahmed.

". . . To which you are all invited. Now," Ilka said in the too-bright voice of a hostess trying to make a sluggish dinner party go, "what shall we talk about? Doesn't do me a bit of good, I know, to ask you all to come forward and sit in a nice cozy clump."

Matsue, an older Japanese from the university's engineering department, sat in his place by the window; Izmira, the Cypriot doctor, had left the usual two empty rows between herself and Ahmed, the Turk. Juan, the Basque, sat in the rightmost corner and Eduardo, the Spaniard from Madrid, in the leftmost. "Who would like to start us off? Somebody tell us a story. Everybody likes stories. Tell the class how you came to America."

The teacher looked determinedly past the hand, the arm, with which Gerti Gruner stirred the air—death, taxes, and Thursdays, Gerti Gruner in the front row center. Ilka's eye passed mercifully over Paulino, who sat in the last row, with his back to the wall. Matsue smiled pleasantly at Ilka and shook his head. He meant "Please, not me!" Ilka looked around for someone too shy to self-start who might enjoy talking if called upon, but Gerti's hand stabbed the air immediately under the teacher's chin, so Ilka said, "Gerti wants to start. Go, Gerti. When did you come to the United States?"

"In last June," said Gerti.

Ilka corrected her, and said, "Tell the class where you are from, and, everybody, please speak in whole sentences."

Gerti said, "I have lived twenty years in Uruguay and before in Vienna."

"We would say, *'Before that I lived'*," said Ilka, and Gerti said, "And *before that* in Vienna."

Ilka corrected her. Gerti's story bore a family likeness to the teacher's own superannuated, indigestible history of being sent out of Hitler's Europe as a child.

Gerti said, "In the Vienna train station has my father told to me . . ."

"*Told me.*"

"*Told me* that so soon as I am coming to Montevideo . . ."

Ilka said, "*As* soon as I *come*, or more colloquially *get* to Montevideo . . ."

Gerti said, "*Get* to Montevideo, I should tell to all the people . . ."

Ilka corrected her. Gerti said, ". . . tell all the people to bring out my father from Vienna before come the Nazis and put him in concentration camp."

Ilka said, "In *the* or *a* concentration camp."

"Also my mother," said Gerti, "and my Opa, and my Oma, and my Onkel Peter, and the cousins Hedi and Albert and Roserl. My father has told, 'Tell to the foster mother, "Go, please, with me, to the American consulate.'"""

"My father went to the American consulate," said Paulino, and everybody turned and looked at him. Paulino's voice had not been heard in class since the first Thursday, when Ilka had got her students to go around the room and introduce themselves to one another. Paulino had said his name was Paulino Patillo and that he was born in Bolivia. Ilka was charmed to realize it was Danny Kaye of whom Paulino reminded her—fair, curly, middle-aged, smiling. He came punctually every Thursday—a very sweet, perhaps a very simple man.

Ilka said, "Paulino will tell us his story *after* Gerti has finished. How old were you when you left Europe?" Ilka asked, to reactivate Gerti, who said, "Eight years," but she, and the rest of the class, and the teacher herself, were watching Paulino put his right hand inside the left breast pocket of his jacket, withdraw a legal-size envelope, turn it upside down, and shake out onto the desk before him a pile of news clippings. Some looked new, some frayed and yellow; some seemed to be single paragraphs, others the length of several columns.

"And so you got to Montevideo . . . ," Ilka prompted Gerti.

"And my foster mother has fetched me from the ship. I said, 'Hello, and will you please bring out from Vienna my father before come the Nazis and put him in—*a* concentration camp!" Gerti said triumphantly.

Paulino had brought the envelope close to his eye and was looking inside. He inserted a forefinger, loosened something that was stuck, and shook out a last clipping. It broke at the fold when

Paulino flattened it onto the desk top. Paulino brushed away some paper crumbs before beginning to read: "La Paz, September 19."

"Paulino," said Ilka, "you must wait till Gerti is finished."

But Paulino read, "Señora Pilar Patillo has reported the disappearance of her husband, Claudio Patillo, after a visit to the American consulate in La Paz on September 15."

"Go on, Gerti," said Ilka.

"The foster mother has said, 'When comes home the Uncle from the office, we will ask.' I said, 'And bring out, please, also my mother, my Opa, my Oma, my Onkel . . .'"

Paulino read, "A spokesman for the American consulate contacted in La Paz states categorically that no record exists of a visit from Señor Patillo within the last two months . . ."

"Paulino, you really *have* to wait your turn," Ilka said.

Gerti said, "'Also the cousins.' The foster mother has made such a desperate face with her lips so."

Paulino read, "Nor does the consular calendar for September show any appointment made with Señor Patillo. Inquiries are said to be under way with the consulate at Sucre." And Paulino folded his column of newsprint and returned it with delicate care into the envelope.

"O.K., thank you, Paulino," Ilka said.

Gerti said, "When the foster father has come home, he said, 'We will see, tomorrow,' and I said, 'And will you go, please, with me, to the American consulate?' and the foster father has made a face."

Paulino was flattening a second column of newsprint on the desk before him. He read, "New York, December 12 . . ."

"*Paulino*," said Ilka, and caught Matsue's eye. He was looking expressly at her. He shook his head ever so slightly and with his right hand, palm down, he patted the air three times. In the intelligible language of charade with which humankind might have frustrated God at Babel, Matsue was saying, "Let him finish.

Nothing you can do is going to stop him." Ilka was grateful to Matsue.

"A spokesman for the Israeli Mission to the United Nations," read Paulino, "denies a report that Claudio Patillo, missing after a visit to the American consulate in La Paz since September 15, is en route to Israel . . ." Paulino finished reading this column also, folded it into the envelope, unfolded the next column and read, "U.P.I., January 30. The car of Pilar Patillo, wife of Claudio Patillo, who was reported missing from La Paz last September, has been located at the bottom of a ravine in the eastern Andes. It is not known whether any bodies were found inside the wreck." Paulino read with the blind forward motion of a tank that receives no message from the sound or movement in the world outside itself. The students had stopped looking at Paulino; they were not looking at the teacher. They looked into their laps. Paulino read one column after the other, returning each to his envelope before he took the next, and when he had read and returned the last, and returned the envelope to his breast pocket, he leaned his back against the wall and turned to the teacher his sweet, habitual smile of expectant participation.

Gerti said, "In that same night have I woken up . . ."

"*I woke* up," the teacher helplessly said.

"*Woke* up," Gerti Gruner said, "and I have thought, What if it is even now, this exact minute, that one Nazi is knocking at the door, and I am here lying not telling to anybody anything, and I have stood up and gone into the bedroom and woke up the foster mother and the foster father, and next morning has the foster mother gone with me to the refugee committee, and they have found for me another foster family."

"Your turn, Matsue," Ilka said. "How, when, and why did you come to the States? We're going to help you!" Matsue's written English was flawless, but he spoke with an accent that was well nigh impenetrable. His contribution to class conversation always involved a communal interpretative act.

"Aisutudieddu attoza unibashite innu munhen," Matsue said.

A couple of stabs and Eduardo, the Madrileño, got it: "You studied at the university in Munich!"

"You studied acoustics?" ventured Izmira, the Cypriot.

"The war trapped you in Germany?" proposed Ahmed, the Turk.

"You have been working in the ovens?" suggested Gerti, the Viennese.

"Acoustic ovens?" marveled Ilka. "Do you mean stoves? Ranges?"

No, what Matsue meant was that he got his first job with a Munich firm employed in soundproofing the Dachau ovens so that what went on inside them could not be heard on the outside. "I made the tapes," said Matsue. "Tapes?" they asked him. They got the story figured out: Matsue had returned to Japan in 1946 and collected his "Hiroshima tapes." He had been brought to Washington as an acoustical consultant to the Kennedy Center, and been hired to come to Concordance to design the sound system of the New Theater, subsequently accepting a research appointment in the department of engineering. He was going to return home, having finished his work—Ilka thought he said—on the reverse bug.

Ilka said, "I thought, ha ha, you said 'the reverse bug'!"

"The reverse bug" was what everybody understood Matsue to say that he had said. With his right hand he performed a row of air loops, and, pointing at the wall behind the teacher's desk, asked for, and received, her O.K. to explain himself in writing on the blackboard.

Chalk in hand, he was eloquent on the subject of the regular bug, which can be introduced into a room to relay to those outside what those inside would prefer them not to hear. A sophisticated modern bug, explained Matsue, was impossible to locate and deactivate. Buildings had had to be taken apart in order to rid them of alien listening devices. The reverse bug, equally impossible to locate and deactivate, was a device whereby those outside were able to relay into a room what those inside would prefer not to have to hear.

"And how would such a device be used?" Ilka asked him.

Matsue was understood to say that it could be useful in certain situations to certain consulates, and Paulino said, "My father went to the American consulate," and put his hand into his breast pocket. Here Ilka stood up, and, though there were still a good fifteen minutes of class time, said, "So! I will see you all next Thursday. Everybody—be thinking of subjects you would like to talk about. Don't forget the symposium tomorrow evening!" and she walked quickly out the door and drove herself home.

Ilka entered the New Theater late and was glad to see Matsue sitting on the aisle in the second row from the back with an empty seat beside him. The platform people were settling into their places. On the right an exquisite golden-skinned Latin man was talking in the way people talk to people they have known a long time with a heavy, rumpled man, whom Ilka pegged as Israeli. "Look at the thin man on the left," Ilka said to Matsue. "He has to be from Washington. Only a Washingtonian's hair gets to be that particular white color." Matsue laughed. Ilka asked him if he knew who the woman with the oversized glasses and the white hair straight to the shoulders might be, and Matsue said something that Ilka did not understand. The rest of the panelists were institute people, Ilka's colleagues—little Joe Bernstine, Yvette Gordot, and Director Leslie Shakespeare in the moderator's chair.

Leslie had the soft weight of a man who likes to eat and the fine head of a man who thinks. Ilka watched him fussing with the microphone. "Why do we need this?" she could read his lips saying. "I thought we didn't need microphones in the New Theater?" Now he quieted the hall with a grateful welcome for this fine attendance at a discussion of one of our generation's unmanageable questions—the application of justice in an era of genocides.

Here Rabbi Shlomo Grossman rose from the floor and wished to take exception to the plural formulation: "All killings are not murders; all murders are not genocides."

Leslie said, "Shlomo, could you hold your remarks until question time?"

Rabbi Grossman said, "Remarks? Is that what I'm making? Remarks! The death of six million—is it in the realm of a question?"

Leslie said, "I give you my word that there will be room for the full expression of what you want to say when we open the discussion to the floor." Rabbi Grossman acceded to the evident desire of the friends sitting near him that he should sit down.

Director Leslie Shakespeare gave a brief account of the combined federal and private funding that had enabled the Concordance Institute to invite these very distinguished panelists to participate in the institute's Genocide Project. "The institute has a long-standing tradition of 'debriefings' in which the participants in a project that is winding down sum up their thinking for the members of the institute, the university, and the public. But this evening's panel has agreed, by way of an experiment, to talk in an informal way of our notions, of the history of the interest each of us brings to this question—problem—at the point of entry. I want us to interest ourselves in the nature of *inquiry*: will we come out with our original notions reinforced? modified? made over?

"I imagine that this inquiry will range somewhere between the legal concept of a statute of limitations that specifies the time within which human law must respond to a specific crime, and the biblical concept of the visitation of punishment of the sins of the fathers upon the children. One famous version plays itself out in the *Oresteia*, where a crime is punished by an act that is itself a crime and punishable, and so on, down the generations. Enough.

Let me introduce our panel, whom it will be our very great pleasure to have among us in the coming month."

The white-haired man turned out to be the West German ex-
mayor of Obernpest, Dieter Dobelmann. Ilka felt the prompt
conviction that she had known all along—that one could tell at a
mile—that that mouth, that jaw, had to be German. The woman
with the glasses was on loan to the institute from Georgetown
University ("There! She's acquired that white hair!" Ilka whis-
pered to Matsue, who laughed.) She was Jerusalem-born Shulamit
Gershon, professor of international law, and advisor to Israel's on-
going project to identify Nazi war criminals and bring them to
trial. The rumpled man was the English theologian Paul Thayer.
The Latin really was a Latin—Sebastian Maderiaga, who was taking time off from his consulate in New York. Leslie squeezed up
his eyes to see past the stage lights into the well of the New Theater. There was a rustle of people turning to locate the voice that
had said, "My father went to the American consulate," but it
seemed to be going to say nothing further and the audience settled back. Leslie introduced Yvette and Joe, the institute's own
fellows assigned to Genocide.

Ilka and Matsue were watching Paulino across the aisle. Paulino
was withdrawing his envelope from out of his breast pocket and
upturned the envelope onto the slope of his lap. The young student sitting beside him got on his knees to retrieve the sliding
batch of newsprint and held onto it while Paulino arranged his
coat across his thighs to create a surface.

"My own puzzle," said Leslie, "with which I would like to puzzle our panel, is this: Where do I, where do we all, get these feel-
ings of moral malaise when wrong goes unpunished and right
goes unrewarded?"

Paulino had brought his first newspaper column up to his eyes
and read, "La Paz, September 19. Señora Pilar Patillo has reported the disappearance of her husband, Claudio Patillo . . ."

"Where," Leslie was saying, "does the human mind derive its expectation of a set of consequences for which it finds no evidence in nature or in history, or in looking around its own autobiography? . . . Could I *please* ask for quiet from the floor until we open the discussion?" Leslie was once again peering out into the hall.

The audience turned and looked at Paulino reading, "Nor does the consular calendar for September show any appointment . . ." Shulamit Gershon leaned toward Leslie and spoke to him for several moments while Paulino read, "A spokesman for the Israeli Mission to the United Nations denies a report . . ."

It was after several attempts to persuade him to stop that Leslie said, "Ahmed? Is Ahmed in the hall? Ahmed, would you be good enough to remove the unquiet gentleman as gently as necessary force will allow. Take him to my office, please, and I will meet with him after the symposium."

Everybody watched Ahmed walk up the aisle with a large and sheepish-looking student. The two lifted the unresisting Paulino out of his seat by the armpits and carried him reading, "The car of Pilar Patillo, wife of Claudio Patillo . . ." backward, out of the door.

The action had something about it of the classic comedy routine. There was a cackling, then the relief of general laughter. Leslie relaxed and sat back, understanding that it would require some moments to get the evening back on track, but the cackling did not stop. Leslie said, "Please." He waited. He cocked his head and listened: It was more like a hiccupping that straightened and elongated into a sound drawn on a single breath. Leslie looked at the panel. The panel looked. The audience looked around. Leslie bent his ear down to the microphone. It did him no good to tap it, to turn the button off and on, put his hand over the mouthpiece, to bend down as if to look it in the eye. "Anybody know—is the sound here centrally controlled?" he asked. The noise was growing incrementally. Members of the audience drew their heads back and down into their shoulders. It came to them—it became impossible to not know—that it was not laughter to which they were listening but somebody yelling. Somewhere there was a person, and the person was screaming.

Ilka looked at Matsue, whose eyes were closed. He looked an old man.

The screaming stopped. The relief was spectacular, but lasted only for that same unnaturally long moment in which a bawling child, having finally exhausted its strength, is only fetching up new breath from some deepest source for a new onslaught. The howl resumed at a volume that was too great for the small theater; the human ear could not accommodate it. People experienced a physical distress and put their hands over their ears.

Leslie had risen. He said, "I'm going to suggest an alteration in the order of this evening's proceedings. Why don't we clear the hall—everybody, please, move into the lounge, have some wine, have some cheese while we locate the source of the trouble."

Quickly, while people were moving along their rows, Ilka popped out into the aisle and collected the trail of Paulino's news clippings. The student who had sat next to Paulino retrieved and handed her the envelope. Ilka walked down the hall in the direction of Leslie Shakespeare's office, diagnosing in herself an inappropriate excitement at having it in her power to throw light.

Ilka looked into Leslie's office. Paulino sat on a hard chair with his back to the door, shaking his head violently from side to side. Leslie stood facing him. He and the panelists, who had disposed themselves around his office, were screwing their eyes up as if wanting very badly to shut every bodily opening through which the understanding receives unwanted information. The intervening wall had somewhat modified the volume, but not the variety—length, pitch, and pattern—of the sounds that continually altered as if in response to a new and continually changing cause.

Leslie said, "Mr. Patillo, we need you to tell us the source of this noise so we can turn this off."

Paulino said, "It is my father screaming."

"Or my father," said Ilka.

Leslie said, "Mr. Patillo is your student, no? He won't tell us how to locate the screaming."

"He doesn't know," Ilka said. She followed the direction of Leslie's eye. Maderiaga was perched with a helpless elegance on the corner of Leslie's desk, speaking Spanish into the telephone. Through the open door that led into Wendy's outer office, Ilka saw Shulamit Gershon hanging up the phone. She came back in and said, "Patillo is the name this young man's father adopted from his second wife who was Bolivian. He's Klaus Herrmann, who headed the German Census Bureau. After the *Anschluss* they sent him to Vienna to put together the registry of Jewish names and addresses, then to Budapest and so on. After the war we traced him to La Paz. I think he got in trouble with some mines or weapons deals. We put him on the back burner when it turned out the Bolivians were after him as well."

Maderiaga hung up and said, "Hasn't he been the busy little man! My office is going to check if it's the Gonzales people who got him for expropriating somebody's tin mine, or the RRN. If they suspect Patillo of connection with the helicopter crash that killed President Barrientos, they'll have killed him more or less."

"My father is screaming," said Paulino.

"This is nothing to do with his father," said Ilka. While Matsue was explaining the reverse bug on the blackboard, Ilka had grasped the principle that disintegrated now that she tried to explain it to Leslie. She was distracted by a retrospective image: Last night, hurrying down the corridor, Ilka had turned and must have seen, since she was now able to recollect, Ahmed and Matsue walking together, in the other direction. If Ilka had thought them an odd couple, the thought, having nothing to feed on, died before her lively wish to maneuver Gerti and Paulino into one elevator before the doors closed so she could come down in the other. Now she asked Ahmed, "Where did you and Matsue go after class last night?"

Ahmed said, "He needed me to unlock the New Theater for him."

Leslie said, "Ahmed, sorry to be ordering you around, but will you go and find Matsue and bring him here to my office?"

"He has gone," said Ahmed. "I saw him leave by the front door with a suitcase on wheels."

"Matsue is going home," said Ilka. "He has finished his job."

Paulino said, "It is my father."

"No, it's not, Paulino," said Ilka. "Those screams are from Dachau and from Hiroshima."

"That is my father," said Paulino, "and my mother screaming."

Leslie asked Ilka to come with him to the airport. They caught up with Matsue queuing, with only five passengers ahead of him, to enter the gangway to the plane.

Ilka said, "Matsue, you're not going away without telling us how to shut that thing off."

Matsue said, "Itto dozunotto shattoffu."

Ilka and Leslie said, "Excuse me?"

With the hand that was not holding his boarding pass, Matsue performed a charade of turning a faucet and he shook his head. Ilka and Leslie understood him to be saying, "It does not shut off." Matsue stepped out of the line, kissed Ilka on the cheek, stepped back, and passed through the door.

When Concordance Institute takes hold of a situation it deals humanely with it. Leslie found funds to pay a private sanitarium to evaluate Paulino. Back at the New Theater, the police, a bomb squad, and a private acoustics company that Leslie hired from

Washington set themselves to locate the source of the screaming. Leslie looked haggard. His colleagues worried when their director, a sensible man, continued to blame the microphone after the microphone had been removed and the screaming continued. The sound seemed not to be going to loop back to any familiar beginning so that the hearers might have become familiar—might in a manner of speaking have made friends—with some one particular roar or screech, but to be going on to perpetually new and fresh howls of agony.

Neither the Japanese embassy in Washington, nor the American embassy in Tokyo got anywhere with the tracers sent out to locate Matsue. Leslie called in the technician. The technician had a go at explaining why the noise could not be stilled. "Look into the wiring," Leslie said and saw in the man's eyes the look that experts wear when they have explained something and the layman repeats what he said before the explanation. The expert had another go. He talked to Leslie about the nature of sound; he talked about cross-Atlantic phone calls and about the electric guitar. Leslie said, "Could you check *inside* the wiring?"

Leslie fired the first team of acoustical experts, found another company and asked them to check inside the wiring. The new man reported back to Leslie: He thought they might start by taking down the stage portion of the theater. If the sound people worked closely with the demolition people, they might be able to avoid having to mess with the body of the hall.

The phone call that Maderiaga had made on the night of the symposium had, in the meantime, set in motion a series of official acts that were bringing to America—to Concordance—Paulino Patillo's father, Klaus Herrmann/Claudio Patillo. The old man was eighty-nine, missing an eye by an act of man and a lung by an act of God. On the plane he suffered a collapse and was rushed from the airport straight to Concordance Medical Center.

Rabbi Grossman walked into Leslie's office and said, "What am I hearing! You've approved a house, on this campus, for the accomplice of the genocide of Austrian and Hungarian Jewry?"

"And a private nurse," said Leslie.

"Are you out of your mind?" asked Rabbi Grossman.

"Almost," Leslie said.

"You look terrible," said Shlomo Grossman, and sat down.

"What," Leslie said, "am I the hell to do with an old Nazi who is postoperative, whose son is in the sanitarium, who doesn't know a soul, doesn't have a dime, doesn't have a roof over his head?"

"Send him home to Germany," shouted Shlomo.

"I tried. Dobelmann says they won't recognize Claudio Patillo as one of their nationals."

"So send him to his comeuppance in Israel!"

"Shulamit says they're no longer interested, Shlomo! They have other things on hand!"

"Put him back on the plane and turn it around."

"For another round of screaming? Shlomo!" cried Leslie, and put up his hands to cover his ears against the noise that, issuing out of the dismembered building materials piled in back of the institute, blanketed the countryside for miles around, made its way down every street of the small university town, into every backyard, and filtered in through Leslie's closed and shuttered windows. "Shlomo," Leslie said, "come over tonight. I promise Eliza will cook you something you can eat. I want you and Ilka— and we'll see who else—to help me think this thing through."

"We know that this goes on whether we are hearing it or not."

"Maggie asked me what it was," said Ilka.

"We—I—" Leslie said, "need to understand how the scream of Dachau is the same, and how it is a different scream from the scream of Hiroshima. And after that I need to learn how to listen to what sounds like the same sound out of the hell in which the torturer is getting what he has coming."

Here Eliza called Leslie. "Can you come and talk to Ahmed?"

Leslie went out and came back carrying his coat. A couple of young punks with an agenda of their own had broken into Herrmann's new American house. They had gagged the nurse and tied her and Klaus up in the new American bathroom. It was here that Ilka began helplessly to laugh. Leslie buttoned his coat and said, "I'm sorry, but I have to go over there. Ilka, Shlomo, I leave for Washington tomorrow, early, to talk to the Superfund people. While I'm there I want to see if I can get funds for a Scream Project . . . Ilka? Ilka, what?" But Ilka had got the giggles and could not answer him. Leslie said, "What I need is for the two of you to please sit down, here and now, and come up with a formulation I can take with me to present to Arts and Humanities."

The Superfund granted Concordance an allowance for Scream Disposal, and the dismembered stage of the New Theater was loaded onto a flatbed truck and driven west. The population along Route 90 and all the way to Arizona came out into the street, eyes squeezed together, heads pulled back and down into shoulders. They buried the thing fifteen feet under, well away from the highway, and let the desert howl.

By Joy Surprised

PICNIC

It was toward the end of the second week, after the second set of experts had failed to find the source of the human howling that emanated from the stage of Concordance University's New Theater, that Joe Bernstine remembered this nice place for a picnic: Get away for an afternoon, grab a break from the scream that could be heard—couldn't *not* be heard—down every street, alley, yard. Shutting doors, closing windows did not prevent the sound from infiltrating the rooms and offices of the institute, the campus buildings, and every store and house in Concordance. It blanketed the countryside for miles around.

Joe and Jenny, young Bethy, little Teddy and his dog Cassandra came in the Bernstines' car; Leslie and Eliza Shakespeare brought

Ilka and her child. Joe put down a blanket for her on the grass. He wanted to be congratulated on discovering this green place in the embrace of a lush little wood. A range of hills separated them from the town.

"From here you can barely hear it," they said.

Ilka sat with Maggie between her legs. Leslie unloaded bags, baskets, boxes, a bucket of ice, more blankets. Joe got the hibachi burning, Jenny unwrapped things and Eliza sliced them. "Leslie, the wine. You know the definition of wine cookery? You drink wine while you cook. Bethy and Teddy, juice? Maggie, an apple."

Ilka said, "Leslie, watch this." The little girl was studying the white little bite she had bitten out of the red apple, bit another bite, studied it and nibbled away the skin that separated the two little bites creating one big bite. She bit another little bite and studied it. "I used to do that!" said Ilka. "The bites are characters in a story." Ilka and Leslie watched Maggie take another and another: one big and three little bites. Ilka and Leslie watched Maggie bite and nibble a family—a community—of apple bites, little, big, and bigger. Eliza and Jenny cooked. Bethy bossed her little brother Teddy so he ran away and chased Cassandra who was barking at the innocent moths. When Joe took Teddy off to play ball, Cassandra barked at the ball. Bethy came and sat on the blanket and bossed little Maggie, who didn't mind.

"Time to eat, everybody." Bethy carried plates, Teddy brought napkins, and Leslie asked if anybody could think of any characters from the bible through Dickens who went to find themselves or ask who they are. They pounced. Everybody got into the discussion. Maggie's eyes stopped looking. Ilka watched the lids incrementally descend and close. Maggie slept. The wind must have changed; the howling from the New Theater might be something out of a nightmare.

Leslie asked Eliza to tell the story about her father and the commencement address.

"My father was the English master at Chapeldown Preparatory School, in Toronto, and his colleagues, the headmaster, and the board were trying to get him to retire. Father failed to understand them by the simple expedient of not hearing what they said. Leslie, you remember that *New Yorker* cartoon? Frame one: Enter pistol-wielding stickup man. Says, 'This is a stickup.' Frame two: People at the bar talking, laughing, drinking. Three: Stickup man shouts, 'This is a stickup!' Four: People at the bar continue talking, laughing, drinking. Frame five: Stickup man shrugs his shoulders, pockets his pistol, and goes away. Father continues going from class to class, teaching English poetry. The headmaster has an idea. He's going to give Dr. Geoffrey—that's my father—the honor of giving the commencement address! The headmaster, in his academic gown, introduces Dr. Geoffrey—their own Dr. Geoffrey who needs no introduction, whose longevity and devotion to Chapeldown School is beyond praise and who will, so sadly, so regrettably, BE RETIRING AFTER GIVING HIS FINAL ADDRESS at these umpteenth Chapeldown Commencement ceremonies! The headmaster urges the boys to give Dr. Geoffrey a well-deserved hand. Applause. An abortive attempt at a standing ovation, some people standing up, some continuing to sit, some standing up and sitting down again. I'm sitting next to mother with the faculty women. We watch father in *his* gown shaking hands with the headmaster who is descending the five steps to the pulpit. Father ascends the pulpit, thanks the headmaster for his kind and generous words, encourages the boys to look up the word *longevity*, reminding them, ha ha ha, of their friend the dictionary, says, 'My address to you today will be short and sweet . . .' Applause in the body of the chapel. Small dogged smile on father's mouth: he is going to get his quotation quoted, 'For "Great is the art of beginning, but greater the art of ending." You can look that up in

Bartlett's Quotations for "By necessity, by proclivity, and by delight, we all quote." Beginnings not endings,' he says is what he has come today to talk about. 'Have any of you, my young friends, given yourselves account of the word *commencement?* Is that not a curious name for a ceremony that concludes the school year for some, for others it is the end of a school career, for yet others the career of a lifetime—of very life! "The hour of departure has arrived, and we go our ways—I to die and you to live. Which is better God only knows," says Socrates.' Joe—is there any of the red wine left in that bottle? Thank you.—'It is not for you, my young friends, to concern yourselves with valedictions, terminations, extinctions, annihilations, quittances—which you can look up in Webster. Look up *curtains, full stops, stubs, nibs, tails, butts, tag* or *fag* ends in Partridge's Dictionary of Slang. To all of you, on this commencement day I say, Hurry up! Begin your holidays, your careers, your adulthood, the rest of your lives this side of eternity. "*O lente, lente, currite noctis equi:* The stars move still, time runs, the clock will strike," and all too soon you too will stand at "the bourn of that country from which no traveler returns." "Death, as the Psalmist saith, is certain to all; all shall die." "From a proud tower in the town Death looks gigantically down." Job says, "There is death in the pot." "Time to be old, To take in sail." "O we can wait no longer, We too take ship, O soul, Joyous, We too launch out on trackless seas, Fearless of unknown shores."' The littlest boys are in an orgy of the fidgets. I said, 'Mother, stop him!' Mother said, 'Exactly how?' 'That's right!' Father says, '"I will encounter darkness as a bride, and hug it in my arms."' The school chaplain—elegant chap, pink cheeks, turned-around collar, beautiful, dove-gray suit, is saying something to the headmaster in the chair next to him and the headmaster gets to his feet. Father is saying, '"I would not live always!" "Soon oh soon shall I sleep in Abraham's bosom." "Dead as a doornail," our ancestors' simile.' Mother and I watch the headmaster. He is walking toward the pulpit. Father says, ' "Sad news, bad news. . . . Through the Persian Gulf, the Red Sea and the Mediterranean—he's dead; . . . The Ahkoond is dead!" "Life and death are equally jests." "There will be one vacant chair." ' The headmaster has arrived at the base of the pulpit, says, 'Thank you so very, very much, Dr. Geoffrey, for your erudite and I must say most moving address . . .' Father says, ' "This dust was once the man." "Close up his eyes and draw the curtain close." "What ugly sights of death within mine eyes!" ' I notice that the chaplain is no longer sitting in *his* chair. Father says, 'It hath often been said . . . "Death in itself is nothing; but we fear to be we know not what, we know not where." And yet "how oft when men are at the point of death have they been merry." ' There is this hefty fellow in overalls—he's walking as if on tiptoe—approaching the pulpit, already got his foot on the first step. Father is saying, ' "What is death after all but sleepe after toile, port after stormie seas, Ease after warre, death after life does greatly please." ' His arms and elbows are warding off the fellow in the overalls pawing at him. The headmaster and the chaplain stand watching from below. The man in overalls pulls, half tumbles Father down the steps. ' "The voice of nature loudly cries, and many a message from the skies, that something in us never dies!" ' cries Father. ' "Death be not proud, though some have called thee Mighty and dreadful, for thou art not so, for those whom thou think'st thou doest overthrow, die not, poor death, nor yet can'st thou kill me!" ' Father shouts. They are hauling him out through the narrow door that I never even noticed to the left of the altar, and the two boys sitting in front of mother get the giggles."

The hills had turned black but not as black as the woods at their backs. The hibachi glowed as the earth's center might glow.

"Look!" Ilka said. Out of the hills galloped danger or was it romance? The two horsemen increased in size, were suddenly here, reining in the mass of horse flesh that reared and beat the air

with hooves. The riders raised wide-brimmed hats to the pic-
nickers on the blankets, turned their steeds and galloped off spurt-
ing clumps of grass, decreased in size, were gone, and Ilka
said, "It's when I'm happy that I want to cry for Jimmy. It's the
woods, hills, the horsemen, the food, stories, talk—being with
you, here with you all. I'm not really crying."

"You are crying." Leslie passed her his handkerchief.

"Did Una ever give you back your handkerchief?" Ilka laughed
and lay back on the blanket. Leslie lay down beside her. A cotton
handkerchief is a poor conductor of heat so that Ilka might mistake the heat where Leslie's palm met hers, the white heat of their
intertwining fingers, for the passage of consolation, but Cassandra barked and barked and barked and barked and barked. Did
Ilka think Leslie's shoulder against her shoulder was the connection of a dear friendship? Ilka was not brave about believing that
she could have what she wanted.

They were sitting up. They were leaving. Must Ilka wake
Maggie or carry her sleeping? Weren't they leaving? Teddy had
brought his little scratchy phonograph. Joe danced with Bethy on
the grass. Bethy was dancing with Teddy who was cutting up.
"Stop it!" she kept telling him, "Stop kidding around!"

"Dance?" Joe Bernstine pulled Ilka to her feet; Ilka felt herself
pressed against his chest where she had never been pressed before. "Not so shabby!" he said to her. Joe and Ilka danced and
turned on the grass, turned past Eliza sitting between Leslie's
knees where Ilka had never seen her sitting before, past smiling
Jenny who held Bethy between her knees, past Maggie asleep on
the blanket. Joe turned and turned Ilka.

Ilka said, "You can, too, hear the sound from Concordance."

Joe said, "Look at Leslie and Eliza dancing!" Leslie was dancing a jig on the grass, hopping from one foot to the other to avoid
the toes of Eliza's sneakers aiming at his ankles, his shins.

Were they leaving? Everybody was standing. Leslie said,
"Everybody will come to our place."

"No they won't," Eliza said, "because I'm going to go to bed."

Unheard of! "Eliza," they teased her, "you never go to bed! Leslie goes to bed. You don't go to bed till dawn. Since when do you go to bed before Leslie?"

Joe said, "Leslie, no fair! You get everybody riled about the bible and Dickens and finding who we are. You never said what you think."

Leslie said, "I think it's a silly question. There is no such 'who.'"

They drove Ilka to her door and Leslie came around to lift sleeping Maggie out of Ilka's lap and carried her up the steps to the front door.

"I can take her," Ilka said,

Leslie said, "I will come by presently."

And now Ilka understood that what she hadn't allowed herself to imagine and had not, consequently, told herself that she desired, was going to come to pass, come to pass tonight. Maggie woke up and cried and had to be jollied and put to bed. Happiness made Ilka deeply patient with so many steps, motions, and revolutions: the opening of drawers and cupboards looking for she couldn't remember what; finding, mislaying and again finding the bottle for Maggie's juice; taking Maggie's shoes off and the socks, seeing the baby turn to stare in the direction of the window: a turn of the wind aggravated the volume and clarity of the human scream—and the child needed to be hugged and tickled to distract her. Ilka unbuttoned and peeled Maggie out of layers of clothing, filled the bath with water, got the temperature right, soaped and rinsed and cuddled her inside the towel, lay beside her incanting one book, another book, the same book another time, every moment distinct and swollen with anticipation.

When the doorbell rang, Ilka, wishing this were any other night and she quiet and decent in her bed, ran down the stairs, opened the door. Leslie stepped inside, closed the door deliberately behind him. He reached for Ilka. "How did this ever happen?" chattered Ilka, ineffably moved by his gravity, his absorption in herself. This was Leslie's hand that traced her arm to the elbow, moved down the length of her back as if over some rare and delicate thing; outlined her arm from the wrist upward; hovered, had an intention. Leslie's hand lay lightly trembling along the side of Ilka's breast. It was Ilka's hand and it was his sex for which she reached.

"Is the baby asleep?" Leslie asked her.

"Yes."

"Shall we go upstairs?"

Ilka walked ahead and turned to ask him, "Are you going to be all right?"

Leslie said, "Yes," and Ilka understood with the tenderest interest that Leslie had had lovers before her.

Leslie asked, "And you?"

"Oh!" said Ilka. "I have nothing to lose."

"Oh, not so!" he said

"This is happening?" said Ilka.

When they lay down with each other, Ilka prevented his motion by raising her head to the window. "Can we do this with that?"

"We can," said Leslie. "The tree may not fall in the forest but whether we hear it or not, the screaming goes on at all times. You know that. What must we wait for?"

With the returned stillness after love, Ilka remembered to worry. "Hadn't you better go?"

"God, no!" said Leslie and drew her against himself and lay so still Ilka thought he slept and got out of her side of the bed, palpated the blackness for her shirt, and reaching the door found it blocked by his body and his appalled voice saying, "Are you going? Where are you going?"

"To check the baby."

"Of course. Go and check the baby. Are you coming back?"

"Yes!"

When he was putting his socks back on Ilka said, "I hope Eliza will not pay for our fun."

Leslie said, "*Will* not. Will *not*."

Ilka was relieved to be clear about this—about anything—and fervently agreed.

"We're too old. There would not be time to recover. I have to be in New York next month. Come with me. Would your mother take care of Maggie?"

On Sunday, Ilka called and Eliza picked up. Ilka said, "There's a razor blade in my throat. Maggie and I better stay home. We shouldn't give you our colds?"

Eliza asked, "Are you in bed?"

"Yes. In bed, no. Yes."

"Leslie and I will come and bring breakfast."

"No!" shouted Ilka. "No, no, no, no. I can't have you bothering. We can come."

Ilka was surprised that Leslie, who opened the door, looked just like Leslie.

Ilka sat at Eliza's kitchen table with her head stupid and stuffed full of cotton wool. The razor blade inside her throat had turned into a flap of skin she could not cough up, or swallow down.

"You look terrible," Eliza told Ilka.

"I am terrible," Ilka said.

Eliza made her hot tea and rum. Eliza said, "I saw the girl in the supermarket. Your mummy must be very, very sick," she said to the little girl on her lap, "or she would be asking 'Which girl?' so she could be seeing the girl's point of view and defending it."

"I'm not defending anybody," said Ilka, her lips thick as if the universal dentist had injected a local paralysis.

Maggie rolled herself up and went to sleep on Eliza's lap. Eliza said, "Why don't Leslie and I keep her overnight, so you can go home and enjoy your cold?"

"No, no, no, no!" shouted Ilka.

On the way home Ilka passed the Bernstines'. Cassandra stood on her hind legs at the iron gate and barked at Ilka.

Institute business sent them on trips. Leslie and Ilka planned dates and times, flights and hotels, and Ilka's mother came and took care of Maggie. "If I let her, she would take her away for good." It shocked Ilka that joy should be so easy. Habit is the enabler.

MISTRAL

Then it was a year since Ilka and Leslie had become lovers. Ilka asked Leslie if he knew how many nights they had got to spend with each other and Leslie folded his hands under his head, computed and named a number.

"That is correct," said Ilka. "When I go to check on Maggie you no longer block the door with your body!"

"I've learned that you will 'slip downstairs and bring us up some chilled white wine and some blue cheese, and crackers, and some fine ruddy-skinned pears,'" quoted Leslie. "I don't think of us as lovers," he said.

"So what are we?"

"Fucking friends."

Ilka, shocked and thrilled at the word in Leslie's mouth, called her friend Jacqueline in New York and told her that Leslie thought they were fucking friends.

"Does he?" said Jacqueline, who had got used to Ilka and her affair. Ilka missed the old greedy interest of Jacqueline's disapproval.

It was Eliza who proposed a holiday together, in Norway maybe. She tended to the North. It fell to Ilka to make inquiries, write the letters: the house she had found was in Provence. "Do you mind?" she asked Eliza.

"You have closed the deal?"

"Actually, yes."

"I mind."

"I'm sorry," said Ilka, and meant it.

They arrived tired and frazzled in the late afternoon and Ilka crossed into a dream of creeping ivy–covered ground and a dovecote and a six-foot topiary egg. The house was stone, severely symmetrical except that the finial urn on the left corner of the rooftop drooped its rim "like melting chocolate," said Eliza.

"Our own Marienbad!" said Ilka.

"Always hated Marienbad," said Eliza.

"It's beautiful, don't you think!" Ilka urged her glum companions. The façade was dappled gold, speckled, striated by age and weather. "Our own Diebenkorn," said Ilka.

They unlocked the door. Ilka's mother said, "For a hundred years has nobody dusted."

Eliza brushed against a wall and came away with a white, with a golden shoulder. "It is returning into its original matter."

Ilka said, "'The ache of antiquity,' Henry James called it."

"The refrigerator is like working hammers," said Ilka's mother.

They had shopped on the way and picnicked at the long deal table. Ilka caressed its gouges and scars. The four grown-ups watched Maggie's head descend and come to rest in the butter. Leslie carried the sleeping child up the stairs. Ilka came behind him. He said, "A summer of not making any love, heaven help us!"

"Oh but the happiness of knowing you are in the house, to expect—to see you—walking into the room . . ."

"Ah," said Leslie.

"Leslie, don't *you* think it's beautiful here?"

"There's only one bathroom," said Leslie.

"Eliza and Leslie, why don't you take the front room," proposed Ilka. "Maggie and I can sleep in here. Mum, how's this for you? Apple trees standing in rows outside your window."

Ilka's mother said, "The bathroom shower goes down by a hole in the tiles."

"Which are all the earth colors with sky blue lozenges! This wallpaper is original I bet you."

"It's curling off the walls," said Eliza. "The mattresses are kapok, knots and craters. I cannot sleep here."

Now Ilka's stomach knotted.

During that first restless night, the ancient Verquières refrigerator sighed before hammering into its active cycles. In the morning the Verquières shower refused hot water to any American who rose after 7 A.M.

Ilka took Maggie into the garden. Shuffle, shuffle, shuffle, Maggie! The ivy was sere. It was the color, and made the sound, of packing paper. Ilka and Maggie shuffled around the topiary egg and round and round the dovecote. Only Ilka loved the liquid monotony of the cooing white birds. They lifted, at intervals, all together, raising a rusty cloud and beating it with wings.

Eliza sent Ilka and Leslie to the village to look for milk. "Flora and I will make the lunch."

"She doesn't let me do anything," complained Ilka's mother. "Don't worry about it," said Ilka and saw her mother was going to chafe and to worry. Ilka and Leslie, with Maggie riding his shoulders, had returned bringing milk, a four-foot baguette, and local information. They had counted the thirty-four houses remaining after the Albergencian massacre of 1345 from which the village had never recovered. "Madame Chelan, the baker, says our topiary egg is the monument to the present owner's mother, who is buried underneath."

"That's nice," said Eliza.

The five of them drove around the country. "Maggie watch the water!" The amenable little girl turned her head toward the narrow, sparkling canal along the left side of the lane. Not once did they meet another car. "Wave, Maggie." Maggie waved to the pair of sad-eyed, brown men who effaced themselves into the hedge.

"Cezanne country, the colors of our tiles!" To the west a wall of rock reared out of the flat, ochre landscape. Here and over there a row of candle-straight trees, planted shoulder to shoulder, formed fences against the prevailing wind, and the rows of perfectly spaced apple trees stood under the sun on single legs upraising patient, fruit-laden arms.

Eliza went up to bed early. Leslie wanted Ilka to come out into the garden but she said, "I promised Maggie I'd read her a story. " "I will read her," said Ilka's mother, but Ilka said, "I promised her." Making love in the garden frightened Ilka. The next day she suggested the little Verquières hotel, but Leslie said, "I would be so embarrassed, I couldn't do anything." Ilka and Leslie sat at the long wooden table together. She liked to talk about their bad behavior. Leslie did not. "You don't think we are dreadful?"

"One must live, to live," Leslie said.

———

"She let me shell the peas," Ilka's mother reported to Ilka.

At dinner Eliza bad-mouthed Winnie. She told about Winnie covering every surface of the apartment with his papers, before he went to move in with Susanna and left them to take care of his boxes."

"Dear," said Leslie.

"He hates you," Eliza said.

"He does not," said Leslie. "Why does he hate me!"

"One has one's reasons," Eliza said, "to hate you."

"That may be so," said Leslie.

Eliza told the story of Winnie's taking Una to London and, worst of all, bringing her back to Concordance with him. Eliza badmouthed Joe Bernstine. "He made Leslie leave a cozy berth at Oxford . . ."

"He didn't 'make me.'"

"So Leslie could run the institute for him."

"He ran it for twelve years . . ."

"And stopped you from writing your book . . ."

Leslie looked nettled. "I haven't stopped writing."

"So *he* can write *his* book."

On the third morning the bathroom shower stopped yielding anybody water, hot or cold, any time of the day.

"The pain-in-the-neck of antiquity," said Eliza.

The two sad-eyed men who had effaced themselves into the hedge—or it might have been two other sad-eyed men—came to the gate, Algerians looking for work.

At lunch Eliza seemed more excited and angrier and returned to the attack on Winnie, his wives, his boxes, his Nobel acceptance speech composed when he was twenty-three.

"That will do," said Leslie to her.

And taking up with little Una; Winnie skedaddling off to the West Coast on the day they lost the baby.

Leslie sat beside Eliza and ate his soup.

Late that same afternoon, the lush golden day turned a yellow gray. A mortal heat laid itself across the silent, unpeopled lanes, the massacred village, the dead ivy, the house with the melting stone urn and walls returning to the dust from whence they came. Maggie woke late from too long a nap, climbed into her mother's lap, cried and held Ilka in a steel embrace. Something in the distance cried, it wept as if Matsue's howl had followed them home to its European genesis. It was a low whine with a muddy multiplicity of voices like a distant organ. The season's mistral.

Ilka's mother pried the screaming child out of Ilka's arms. "Let's you and me go and play. Let's go. Come."

Eliza stood in the kitchen, her hair on end. Leslie went to her and said, "You can not blow here, with the child. Do you want to go home now?" Eliza picked a glass off the table and threw it at Leslie. It bounced off the back of his hand and shattered on the floor. Eliza went up the stairs into the master bedroom. Leslie followed her but she had shut the door, fastened it on the inside and screamed. Maggie came running and butted her head into Ilka's stomach.

The mistral howled close.

Leslie said to Ilka, "Can you sit with me?"

"Maggie," Ilka said, "*you* get to sleep with Omama Flora! Will that be fun?"

The child burrowed her head under Ilka's arm.

"*Yes*, you want to sleep with Omama," said Ilka. "Yes, yes, yes!"

Leslie and Ilka sat at the table. He said, "You need to find someone who is at liberty to love you."

"Don't!" said Ilka. They sat together through the night. Eliza had become silent but the howling outside did not let up. Ilka's mother, coming down with Maggie the next morning, asked Leslie how he had got the purple bruise that covered the back of his hand.

Leslie said, "I hit it against the door post." He picked Maggie up and set her on his lap but put her down when Eliza came in. She looked rueful, wanted to apologize. Leslie prevented her. "There is nothing for you to apologize for." All day Leslie kept his person beside Eliza, sat, rose, went out, went up the stairs with her.

The mistral whined and would whine for some days after Leslie and Eliza had returned to America.

LESLIE'S SHOES

Ilka didn't see that it was a phallus until she noticed a second one on the left; then she saw the whole row—another row on the right, an avenue of them. She was walking with the Cokers, an elderly couple from her table in the ship's dining room, the second day out, on their third Greek island. Mr. Coker put on his glasses, recognized the five-footer on its stone pedestal, and took his glasses off. He polished them with a white handkerchief, laid them away in their hard case, and said, "Bifocals! Would you believe a hundred bucks?"

"Wow," said Ilka.

"You can say that again!" said Mr. Coker and, shaking his head in admiration, returned the case into his breast pocket. Mrs. Coker carried a large beige bag. Ilka had meant to look at her across the breakfast table, but the eyes refused to focus on Mrs. Coker. Ilka once again dismissed the bizarre notion that Mr. Coker beat Mrs. Coker. We can't deal with other people till we've cut them down to fit some idea about them, thought Ilka, and looked around for anybody to say this to. Ilka's idea about the Cokers was that one didn't tell them one's ideas. She looked at the Cokers to see if they were cutting her down, but she could tell that the Cokers *had* no ideas about her.

Ilka looked over at the American woman, but she was looking through her camera, saying, "Belle, Hank, lovies, go stand over by the left one so I can get in all that sea behind you." The American woman appeared to be traveling with that little bevy of good-looking younger people, but it was her one noticed. One always knew the table at which she sat, not because her voice was loud but because it was fearless. Ilka thought of her as the American woman although many passengers on the British cruise ship *Ithaca* were Americans. Ilka herself was a naturalized American, but this was a tall, slim, fair woman who moved as if gladly, frequently turning her head to look this way and that. She kept generating fresh and always casual and expensive pairs of pastel pants and sweaters.

Ilka stored her idea about the Cokers and her curiosity about the American woman in the back of her mind to tell Leslie, whom she was scheduled to meet in an Athens hotel—a week from yesterday.

In the waiting area at Heathrow, Ilka had checked out the glum, embarrassed passengers with the telltale green flight bags and had yearned toward the interesting English group in the leather chairs by the window—two couples and a beautiful one-armed clergyman. They seemed to know one another. Perhaps they were old friends?

At the Athens airport the green flight-bag people had been transferred onto buses to take them down to the Piraeus, and the

three men from the leather chairs turned out to be the three English scholars who came as part of the package. Professor Charles
Baines-Smith knew what there was to be known about shipbuild-
ing in the ancient Near East; Willoughby Austen had published a
monograph on the identity of the Island of Thera with the lost
island of Atlantis. It was the Reverend Martin Gallsworth who
gave the lecture that first evening, after dinner, as the *Ithaca*
pulled out of the wharf.

Ilka sat in a state of romance. She looked up at the Greek
moon in the Greek sky and across the glittering black strip of the
Aegean to the Attic coast passing on the right. She leaned to hear
what the Reverend Gallsworth was saying about the absence, in
the Hellenic thought system, of the concept of conscience which
the Hebrews were developing in that same historical moment,
some hundred miles to the east.

The two classy Greek women guides assigned to the *Ithaca* did
not appear till breakfast, which they ate at a little table for two.
Dimitra, the elder by ten years, walked with a stick, as if she were
in pain—a small, stout, cultivated woman. Ilka liked her. She as-
sembled the crowd in the foyer between the purser's desk and the
little triangular corner counter where one could buy toothpaste
and postcards of the *Ithaca* riding at anchor or the little square
pool on the upper deck. Ilka sent the *Ithaca* card to everybody at
Concordance.

Dimitra led her little crowd off the boat, got them loaded onto
the waiting buses and unloaded them in the parking lot at the bottom of twin-peaked Mount Euboea. Mycenae! Idea turned earth
underfoot, grass, some wild trees, blue water, blue, blue sky and
a lot of stones: Agamemnon's actual palace! "Mine eyes dazzle,"
Ilka said to the tiny, very very old English woman, bent at a 90
degree angle, who could be trusted not to hear. The old woman
looked as if she needed all her wits to get one foot put in front of
the other. The ascent was hot and steep but the very old English
woman waved her sturdy stick at the campstool that the nice man

with all the cameras offered to unfold for her. She was going to stand like everybody else while Dimitra explained how the pre-Greek *ae* ending told scholars that Mycenae had been inhabited since the early Bronze Age. "That's around 3,000 B.C. Over there is the famous lion gate you see on the postcards."

Mr. Coker took his glasses out of their hard case and looked at them. "Would you believe bifocal *sun*glasses!" he turned to say to the American woman.

"Up there," said Dimitra, "is where—one story says at the table, another one says in his bath—Clytemnestra and her lover Aegisthus murdered the 'king of men,' as Homer calls Agamemnon, on his return from the sack of Troy." When the old English woman raised her head to look, she tumbled, lisle legs and plimsolls in the air, backward into the grave-circle in which, in 1876, the German, Schliemann, thought he had unearthed Agamemnon's golden death mask, tiaras, thoi, bracelets, and a necklace clasped around the cervical of what might have been a Mycenean princess whose royal garments had disintegrated a millennium ago. The old woman flailed her stick at the hands reaching down to her and climbed out by herself.

I think she thinks once she accepts help, she'll lose herself, Ilka was going to tell Leslie in Athens on Tuesday.

"This way, everybody, please!" They stood peering down into the subterranean blackness of the cistern which, in times of siege, had brought water from the well outside the Cyclopean wall into the royal palace. "There are one hundred wet and very worn steps. *Please* let us not have any accidents," said Dimitra, and the very old woman gave herself a small sad smile, a half shake of the head, and turned away. Ilka saw her, later, standing on Agamemnon's flagstones and said, "I think I'm looking for the place where a bloody bath might have actually stood."

Dimitra was clapping her hands. "*Ithaca* people, over here, please!" She kept one hand in the air. Ilka watched her watching the excruciating slowness with which a lot of people form into a group that can be instructed. "Let us not become mixed with the people in the buses from the hotels. We are the green bus."

Day two their guide was Aikaterini, an elegant woman with an interesting air of sorrow, though it might only have been the sorrow of a woman in her fifties. The American woman wore a peach cotton knit sweater tied round her slim waist and looked terrific.

It grew hotter. Sky and water were so blue that the whiteness of the marble columns constituted the dark element. "You're standing on land's end, which would have been the returning sailor's first sight of home." Something for Aikaterini's little group to imagine.

The Reverend Gallsworth with his romantically missing arm was sitting on a stone. Ilka went and sat beside him and said, "This is embarrassing!"

The Reverend Gallsworth looked suspicious.

"Here I was being all dazzled and this turns out not to even be the original Temple of Poseidon after all! Darn thing is a mere thousand years old!" Ilka was flirting with the Reverend Gallsworth. The Reverend Gallsworth smiled with an exquisite exhaustion.

Ilka said, "Something I wanted to ask you, about your lecture."

The Reverend Gallsworth looked alarmed.

Ilka said, "Conscience doesn't do a very good job, does it! Sin really is like death: one lives comfortably enough with the knowledge of both for a good twenty-three out of the twenty-four hours."

Here the Reverend Martin Gallsworth looked, and saw Ilka, and Ilka rose, said, "Well, I think I better . . ." and ran away.

Ilka went and stood beside Aikaterini. "I do sympathize with the two of you having to squeeze everything you know into five

minutes spiced up with skeleton princesses and homing sailors."
Ilka was flirting with Aikaterini, who drew her head subliminally
backward. Ilka experienced the thrill of recognition. She said,
"Your head is doing what my head does when one of my students
comes up and asks me something to which the real answer is,
"O.K.! I notice you!"

The sorrowful, elegant Aikaterini did not smile at Ilka.

Ilka saved the head drawing subliminally backward to tell
Leslie.

The sun stood straight above the avenue of the phalli. Ilka
worked her way forward, fell into step beside Dimitra, and tried
again: "I'm getting used to coming to what looks like another lot
of stones, and then you talk for five minutes and the stones stand
up and they're baths, markets . . ."

"Yes?" said Dimitra.

Ilka looked at Dimitra, looked around at all the groups and
guides, looked at the crowd from the *Ithaca*. There was no one
who cared anything about her and Ilka longed for Tuesday. She
wiped the hair out of her damp forehead and looked inside her
bag. No comb. Was that a comb held toward her by the hand of
the American woman? "Keep it," the American woman said. I always travel with two or three. I'm Boots."

"Well, thank you so much! I'm Ilka."

The American woman introduced her nephew, Hank, and his
brand-new wife, Belle. The young people smiled nicely and walked
off together. Boots pointed to a pleasantly ugly man Ilka had noticed. His wide smile was squeezed way down into the lower half
of his face as if he had a secret he might be glad to be rid of. He
turned out not to be Boots's husband, but Boots's husband's baby
brother. "Poor Herbert. His wife died three years ago and he
hasn't got anything going. You must come and sit at our table,"
said Boots.

When Ilka got onto the green bus, Boots was in the first seat on the right and moved over for her. The smiling brother-in-law sat in back with the man with the cameras.

"So which is your husband?" Ilka asked her.

"Oh, Coleman! He's a dear but absolutely unpersuadable on the subject of travel. His birthday present to me is to take Herb and the kids on a Hellenic cruise!"

"Wow," Ilka said.

"And he stays home and plays golf."

"And everybody is happy!" said Ilka.

"Everybody couldn't be happier," said Boots. "Driver, what's holding us up?"

The Greek driver didn't know, but they must stay on the bus and not get off. When they were still standing twenty minutes later, the driver said they could get off, but must not leave the parking area.

"Oh, funsies!" said Boots.

Boots introduced the brother-in-law, who looked at Ilka with a smile inappropriately wide. He introduced the man with the cameras. Ilka had thought he was Jewish but his nose turned out to be a French nose: his name was Marcel. Boots invited him to sit at her table. They stood around the parking lot for the better part of an hour before Dimitra returned: An accident in the Sanctuary of the Bulls. An elderly American had had a heart attack, the wife didn't know what bus they had come on, didn't know the name of the hotel they were staying in. "Horrible—in a foreign place." Dimitra had stayed to help out with the English while they connected with the American consulate.

"Takes the stuffing out of you, that sort of thing," said Boots back in the bus. Ilka was appalled to be telling this woman she didn't know, and didn't necessarily like, about Jimmy's death driving back from Washington.

———

Next morning a mist suffused the brightness. Boots and Ilka leaned on the ship's railing and watched the silver islands on a silver sea, and the ones that were far away and large enough to live on looked the same size as the rocks with their bonsai vegetation passing close at hand.

Close at hand Boots's handsome face was creped and cratered below the corners of the lips—the toll taken by so much slimness?

Why was Ilka telling Boots about Leslie? "There's a gospel song about Jesus when he meets the woman at the well and tells her everything she's done. *'Woman,' said, Woman, you got three husbands but the one you got now isn't yours.'* I had only one husband but this one belongs to a friend."

"Is he cute?" Boots asked Ilka.

"God no!" said Ilka.

"Cole's pretty cute," Boots said.

Ilka hesitated a moment, and another moment, so that when she said, "Leslie," in Boots's presence it had the force of an event. "Leslie and I make these half-assed attempts to stop seeing each other, trusting the other to refuse. Our consciences aren't working very well. So, I left my little girl with my mother . . ."

"You have a child," said Boots and looked as if someone had boxed her ears: the eyes snapped wide, the lips thinned to pencil lines and peeled back from the splendid parade of her teeth.

"My Maggie," said Ilka. "Leslie thinks I need to move on and find someone . . . He told me to come on this cruise. But he's meeting me in Athens. He arranged for our hotel room. Leslie arranged for me to get off the *Ithaca* in Istanbul . . ."

"Coleman is an arranger," said Boots.

Ilka couldn't stop. "I have this theory that the men of feeling and passion . . ."

"No such animal," said Boots.

"Oh, but there is! Only it isn't the ones with the long hair and the jeans, it's the one who keeps his legs inside the stovepipes of his business suit and his throat knotted with a tie till he takes everything off . . ."

"Does Leslie talk?" asked Boots. Ilka was unpleasantly startled to hear his name in Boots's mouth. "Cole never hears a word I say to him."

"Leslie hears what I *mean*," boasted Ilka. Ilka was not hearing what Boots was saying or what Boots meant.

Ilka waved to the Cokers from the table at which she now sat with Boots, the smiling brother-in-law, and the French photographer. The young people had found themselves a table with a lot of other young people. After Professor Baines-Smith's talk on the pumice of Thera, Boots invited him and his wife to sit at her table. He was charming and courteous but continued to sit with the other English experts forming a virtual high table. The two interesting Greek guides continued to sit at their table for two. Boots had gone ahead and acquired the Tottenhams, an English high school teacher of classics with a severe stammer and his clever wife, Dotty, who did his talking for him. Now Boots and her entourage walked together and rested together on a circle of stones. "Look! How Greek!" Boots pointed to a boy hurrying a little mule down a path so steep the animal had no time to place its feet, and the very very old English woman's mouth opened. She said,

"Ah! The poor thing!"

Sunday, and the friends agreed it was a blessed relief to have no excursion planned: into the bus, out of the bus, stand and wait, look left, look up. "And when it is hot," said Marcel, "I can't see anything."

"That's right! Or feel anything! That's true," cried Ilka. "And if you stay back on the boat, you chafe at whatever ancient Greek or new human thing you might be missing out on."

Why was Boots giving Ilka a look?

Around eleven that morning Ilka had passed the open lounge door and seen Boots sitting at the bar. She went in. "This is Aziz," Boots said. Ilka knew Aziz, who had trimmed her hair in the ship's tiny barbershop. He was lovely looking if you liked your men young with soft eyes, a chiseled nose, a pure jawline, and a childish back of the neck.

"Coleman's an absolute dear," Boots was telling the young man, "but un-per-*sua*-dable on the subject of travel. Our house backs onto the golf course. Cole steps out the door and is *on* the golf course." It was not clear to Ilka if young Aziz understood what Boots was saying to him. He smiled and looked apprehensively in the direction of the door. The ship's staff were not supposed to hobnob with the guests. "I'll take another." The elderly waiter behind the bar put down his Greek newspaper. "And one for my friend, here. No? Why not? What? What are you looking at your watch for?" Boots asked Ilka. "We know *you* don't always play by the rules."

Ilka was shocked by the hatchet in Boots's voice.

Boots said, "Tomorrow night Aziz is going to show us the real Istanbul. Listen! I'll square it with the powers that be."

"Yes, I show you!" the young man said, with an eye on the door. "I have friend is chauffeur. He borrows one car. A friend from his friend is waiter in restaurant on the water, beautiful. I take you to Asia. I show you." The lounge door opened, the boy jumped. Boots said, "You're making me nervous. Go, go, go, go. We make arrangements. Come to my cabin."

The ship was scheduled to pass Haghia Sophia at the moment of sunrise. Boots's young folks refused to so much as think about getting up. The rest of the friends asked the steward to rouse them, but only Marcel, Herbert, and Ilka rose when roused. They, the very old English woman with her cane, Mr. Coker with his bifocals, and a half-dozen other passengers stood on the captain's deck. Ilka shivered. Herbert put his jacket around her shoulders and kept his arms around his jacket with Ilka inside.

"Thank you! Oh, wow! Look at that! Oh!"

"Like a picture postcard," someone said.

Oh, lucky Marcel! He had something he could do about beauty—focus, frame it and snap! Have it to take home! How was Ilka to tell Leslie about this silhouette of domes passing the yellow heart of light?

Boots, Ilka, clever Dotty Tottenham, and the nephew and his pretty wife did the bazaars. The hope of treasure is coeval with love and sin. Boots bought the latest guidebook, called *Turkey Traversed.* After lunch she and Tom Tottenham and his Michelin sat on deck by the little swimming pool, blue as an upward-looking eye, and decided where Aziz was going to take them. Marcel leaned over the railing and took pictures of the little jolly boats that chugged around the sunny water like the bumper cars in a funhouse.

Aziz met them round a corner out of the sightlines of the powers that be. He was excited, looked charming, had a car and a friend twice his age and inclining to fat, who had another car.

The two cars shone blackly in the Turkish night. Boots and Tom Tottenham sat in back urging the advice in their own guidebook against the advice in the other's guidebook. Boots said, "Listen to this: 'The Khedive Sarai, or Palace Khedive, home of the last Ottoman Pasha of Egypt, has been turned into a cafe!'" But Aziz had already told the other car where to rendezvous.

"Aziz! This is adorable!"

The charming restaurant, the lights, their own upside-down reflection in the black water. A young waiter in black and golden tights came with a single long-stemmed scarlet rose for each lady. Another waiter brought a platter with an enormous fish.

"How you call in America *levrek?*"

"Search me," said Boots.

More young black and golden men came—or it might have been one or maybe two young men who kept coming—carrying mussels cooked with rice and berries stuffed back into their shells; with stuffed vine leaves, eggplant; with egg rolls filled with white cheese and meat, a mixture of mushroom, tomatoes, and peas. Aziz sat by Boots and taught her the names of the dishes and how to pronounce them. There came bottles—"*Ouzo,*" said Aziz. "*Raki.*" Tomorrow night Ilka was going to tell Leslie about the blanched, sumptuous, crisply tender, larger-than-life almonds floating in their clear liquid in a silver dish.

Boots said, "Aziz, how far is it to this Khedive? Listen: '. . . home of the last Ottoman Pasha of Egypt has been turned into a cafe from which the visitor can enjoy one of finest views of the Golden Horn.'"

Aziz said, "I think I regret is closed the Khedive Cafe. I have arranged for you hookahs."

"How many people want hookahs and how many would rather go to the Khedive?"

Dotty Tottenham said, "Boots, it's all been arranged . . ."

"How far is it to the hookahs?" asked Boots as they got back into the two cars. Not at all far up the shore road they got out, and Aziz walked them into a terraced, outdoor establishment. They were introduced to the problematic of the hookah, a fat glass bottle Ilka remembered from a child's picture book of the fat thief of Baghdad. Aziz, the friend, and the friend who owned the establishment went from guest to guest, showed them how to blow and ran to untie those who got themselves entangled in the ingoing and outcoming tubes. A lot of good-natured laughter turned to discouragement, to boredom. How about the Khedive?

They got back into the cars and drove up and up and up and there was the view, but the Cafe Khedive was in darkness.

Boots said, "But I need to pee! Too much ouzo and, Aziz, what was that other drink supposed to be called?" Aziz and his friend were arguing with a person—a man—whom they had roused and who stood blocking the entrance to the cafe. "What the hell, I'm going to pee!" said Boots, and that, Ilka told Leslie, was the high point of the night—that communal peeing in the warm Turkish darkness with the Bosporus way, way below and the long arrow straightness of the bridge which they had crossed from Europe to Asia.

Some of the party were ready to return to the boat. Ilka, scheduled to disembark before breakfast, hadn't finished her packing, but Boots wanted one more drink. Aziz and the friend consulted. They knew an all-night place. "There is where is the best singer of my country's music."

"Not too far is it, Aziz?" asked Boots. "Where the hell are they taking us? I hope he knows where he's going. Aziz, sweetie, why are you taking us out into the boondocks? Where the hell are we?"

It was a barn of a restaurant and they were the only patrons. The table was not big enough for their party, so Aziz and his friend and the proprietor sat at another table. The lone singer on the wooden platform accompanied himself with a steady driving beat on a curious stringed instrument. Herb sat beside Ilka, and Ilka said, "If he were American he'd be tossing his hips and showing his glottis, and yet he gets in the same amount of sex standing ramrod straight and sliding his tones like diphthongs."

Boots said, "What's wrong with tossing your hips?"

"I didn't say there was anything wrong . . ."

"I didn't say you did," said Boots, "but yougotchawatchout for people putting America down."

"I wasn't putting it down," lied Ilka. "I meant some cultures do things one way and some another, which is interesting."

"That's right!" Boots held out her glass and said, "Gimme one more whatchucallit. Like some women flash their ankles, and some women flash their smarts."

Ilka reddened and said, "That's true! That's just what I do! That's clever of you!" She looked at Boots with surprised admiration.

Boots said, "Gotchawatchout for people with their vocabulary walking off with other people's husbands."

Ilka blinked, looked and was staring down the two sheer abysses of Boots's pale eyes that had no bottom, and no surface from which Ilka could have caught the rebound of something as distinct as hatred.

Ilka sat in the car, silent, her throat blocked while the well-bred Dotty Tottenham persevered in worrying about her lawn, which she had left in the care of a friend's son home for the hols. Ilka was subliminally grateful for the warmth of Herbert's thigh alongside her own. In her imagination Ilka was explaining herself to Boots: "You're accusing me of something *I* accused *myself* of. You're using ammunition that I gave you, against me. And what good does it do *you* to squeeze *me* into the narrowest idea of me?" Ilka longed for Leslie. Ilka tried to think that Boots had not meant what Boots had meant.

The *Ithaca* lay asleep in the cradling water. The little foyer, empty except for their drunken, yawning selves, looked seedy. Had the light in here always been so brown? The marbleized linoleum was all worn in front of the purser's desk and in front of the triangular corner counter.

Boots said, "I'm dead. Aziz, that was a really great, great, great evening. You're an ab-so-lute love! Listen, what do we owe you?"

The stout friend was gone. Aziz drew up his slender young person, threw his head back and laid his hand upon his heart. "You are my guests, the guests of my country."

"Don't be silly," said Boots. "I don't know what you make, but I can just about imagine it's not enough to take eight people out to dinner, and god knows what those cars and hookahs and those roses set you back for. You'd make life a lot easier for everybody if you'd tell us and we'll divvy it up between us and go to bed. Otherwise we're going to stand here till we figure it out which is going to be a real pain."

Aziz kept shaking his head. He covered his eyes with his hand.

Boots said, "I've got my pen. Anybody got a piece of paper?" She and Tom Tottenham leaned their heads over the purser's desk and started counting the dishes in the restaurant on the water plus the ouzo. "Aziz, did we drink two or three bottles of that other thing—what's it called?"

Aziz put his forehead on the counter with the postcards and the toothpaste and covered his ears.

Herbert had got up to say good-bye. Ilka was glad it was so early she would not be likely to see Boots again, but here was Boots with her morning face, in her robe. Boots embraced Ilka, Ilka embraced Boots. They exchanged addresses. Ilka looked back from the little launch chugging through the sheer white dawn and waved to Boots and Herbert waving from the ship's railing.

Leslie had said, "Let's not have confusion. I'll come and meet you when you get through customs. Sit in the waiting area and I will find you."

The area was under reconstruction. A temporary screen cut off Ilka's view of all but the approaching feet. The variety of women's shoes and ankles was an entertainment, but Ilka learned that she wasn't sure she would know Leslie's shoes in a crowd. Did Leslie wear cuffs on his trousers? Ilka could tell those gray ones weren't Leslie: Leslie would not saunter to meet Ilka. And he was too heavy for the bounce of those flannels; that was a young man. The navy pants were running, and Leslie did not run. That pair of good brown shoes, not new, driving at a steady forward pace toward Ilka—Leslie was coming.

An End

YOM KIPPUR CARD

Und doch welch Glück geliebt ʒu werden!
Und lieben, Götter, welch ein Glück!

—from Göthe's "Abschied"

Joe and Jenny Bernstine in Concordance e-mailed Ilka in New York the late-breaking news from the institute: Nat Cohn was reunited—once again—with Nancy. Matsue was back from Japan and sent Ilka his best, at least that's what Joe had understood Matsue to be sending Ilka. Big government grant to study the practical applications of the Reverse Bug. Jenny wrote that Eliza was on the rampage. "She told Zack Zee he had a mouth like a keyhole with the key stuck on the inside. Joe thinks, with Leslie gone, Eliza is bent on shedding one after another of her friends. She's starting on Winterneet."

Eliza Shakespeare phoned Ilka: "Finished off Winnie. I called and told him, 'I hoisted your boxes into the trunk of my car. I'm driving them to the dump.' You," Eliza reminded Ilka, "used to looooove going to the dump with Leslie."

There was nothing, nothing, not any thing that Ilka had not loved doing with Leslie. She said, "It's that weird expanse. It has a disgusting grandeur, don't you think?"

"No," said Eliza.

"With the gulls circling..."

"Scavengers," said Eliza.

"I never understood,"—Ilka had found her side in a nonexistent argument and pounced—"why we are so down on scavengers being ourselves a dead-meat-eating species. Anyway. So. What did Winnie say?"

"Asked me why I was being a bitch. I said, 'Because you took yourself off to Berkeley on the day we lost the baby. And because I need to clear the decks before I can get started on Leslie's manuscript.' How is your mother?" she asked Ilka.

Joe wrote: "Jenny thinks Eliza is waiting for me to offer to turn what Leslie was working on into a publishable manuscript. You saw most of it. Is there enough in any final form?" Ilka wrote back: "I shouldn't think so. The chapters he sent me were the source of a bad argument between us. I hurt him by disagreeing with what he was saying."

Jenny wrote: "Eliza has Leslie's papers spread over the whole dining table."

Ilka phoned Eliza. "How are you coming with Leslie's manuscript?"

"I'm trying to organize the chapters he wrote back in Oxford but I don't understand his code for first, second, and later drafts. Some of it looks more like notes he was writing to himself..."

"Would you like me to come down and help?"

"I don't know what I would like."

Joe wrote: "Eliza told us you offered to come and help her. We would hire you back on a temporary basis." Jenny added, "You could stay with us. Bring Maggie. Bethy wishes she had a little sister like Maggie instead of a stupid, obnoxious, stinky, etc., etc., brother like Teddy."

Joe wrote: "At dinner yesterday, Eliza told Alvin the very rude thing he could do with his perpetual revolution. He just laughed and kissed her hand, but when she asked if Alicia was working on an appropriate cliché, we drove her home."

Ilka wrote them: "Leslie used to say on her bad days Eliza feels that nothing and nobody is any good."

Eliza gave Ilka her version of these events: "Zack sits across the table withholding his disapproval while Alvin promises, come the revolution, rust and moth will cease to corrupt. Poor Alvin. He sees the Thinker's naked concentration furrow Alicia's forehead and goes into hibernation until she's finished talking. Then he opens his eyes and rejoins the conversation." Ilka thought she heard the mistral's distant, dangerous roar in back of Eliza's voice. Eliza said, "How is your mother?"

"Fine."

"How is Maggie?"

"Maggie is fine. Eliza, are you O.K.?"

"Perfectly 'O.K.,' as you so *eloquently* put it. I'm raw as if my skin had been flayed. Bumping into things hurts—bumping into people one hates and there is nobody I don't hate."

"Eliza! You don't hate the Bernstines."

"The Bernstines are golden," said Eliza.

Jenny called. "We worry about her. She starts on her first glass of wine who knows when and sips till she goes to bed if she ever goes to bed. I have to wonder if she eats. Leslie's papers have crept into the foyer, over the console and the chair. Joe wants to talk."

Joe took the phone. "I think that she keeps spreading papers to put off the moment she has to start putting them in order which it's never going to be possible to do. It's really rather a nightmare. Yesterday, she told Nat and Nancy that they disprove Tolstoy's idea about unhappy families all being different because *they* bickered like all the bickering couples one has ever had the misfortune to have to listen to. She's going to run out of people to demolish."

Eliza called Ilka to bad-mouth Joe Bernstine. "He pried us away from Oxford where Leslie could have finished his book. Joe made Leslie come to Concordance to run the institute so Joe could finish *his* book. He won't lift a finger to help me put Leslie's book in shape: 'The hell with Shakespeare. Raise high the Bernstine.'"

Did Ilka hear an anti-Semitic note? Ilka swallowed. She said, "But, Eliza . . ."

"I knew you were going to defend the Bernstine. If you are not on my side, don't talk at all."

"Of course I am on your side, only Leslie agreed to come back. And Joe had been running the institute for over a decade . . ."

Eliza had hung up.

———

Both Bernstines were on the line. "Eliza is not talking to us. I call her," Jenny said, "she picks up and says she's asleep and left a notice not to be disturbed. I call later and she says she is out of town. Think of her alone in that house with those papers."

Joe said, "She called Celie. She's coming to the institute to get the files from Leslie's office. She's going to add the chapters he did in Concordance to aggravate the confusion."

Eliza rang Ilka. "How long were you and Leslie having this hot and heavy affair?"

There are moments when the world stops turning. Such a moment is empty: nothing exists in it. It has a duration and when the world resumes its revolution the direction and everything afterward has been altered. Since the day of the picnic when Leslie and Ilka had made love, she had tried, once in a while, to prepare for this moment. She had attempted various scenarios but the imagination always balked and turned aside before she could think of the words she would speak to Eliza.

Now Ilka said, "It wasn't really, you know."

"Don't deny it."

Ilka said, "I don't." What Ilka had meant by *it wasn't really* was *hot and heavy* but she understood Eliza to have heard *I don't* and *it wasn't* as denials of the fact.

"I hold in my hand the letter you wrote to him. It was in a file in his office at the institute. How many letters did you write him?"

"Filed in error. You were never supposed to see it." Was that strangled sound on the wire a laugh? "You were never supposed to be hurt. That sounds stupid."

"It does," Eliza said. "How long did this affair go on?"

This was not the time to complain how utterly and totally the word *affair* failed to denote Leslie and Ilka's love. Ilka was operating on the principle which experts tell us to remember when answering a child's question about a fact we wish it had not chosen this moment, or any other moment to ask us: don't lie, but don't elaborate, they advise. What we do is work around the enormous central truth. Ilka said, "Stupid or not, his first care was always for you. It really always was."

"This letter in my hand is written in a language I did not imagine to exist until a moment ago," Eliza said and hung up.

Ilka hung up, picked the phone up again, called Jenny and said, "Jenny, please go and look in on Eliza. Please. It may be real real trouble. You don't know but Leslie and I had a—had an affair."

After a moment, Jenny said, "Well, we know that."

"You do? No, you don't! Leslie and I were excruciatingly careful . . . How could you know?"

"The way one knows things. And Eliza told us."

"She didn't. She couldn't, Jenny, she didn't know until a moment ago. She found a letter that got into a file in Leslie's office. I know she didn't know—Jenny, it was her suggestion that Leslie and I travel in Greece together. What makes you think she knew?"

"Well, she didn't know, and yet one night—this is a couple of years back, when she had a lot to drink and was beating up on Leslie, she said 'You're betraying me with an outlander.'"

"With an—oh, I see. I see. What did Leslie say?"

"Leslie said, 'Dear, here is your coat. Say good-bye to Alpha. Say good-bye to Alfred.' Speaking of Alfred, last week, before Eliza stopped talking to us, we had her to dinner with the Stones and Eliza told Alfred when she saw him coming up the street she put her hands out in front of her so as not to run into his glass wall."

"The Stones! Do they . . . does everybody know!"

"Maybe," said Jenny.

"Jenny, go and see if Eliza is O.K."

"She's not going to let me in. But I'll go right away."

"Please, Jenny!"

Ilka hung up the phone. The phone rang. Eliza said, "I don't know how to do this by myself. I can't do this. Help me."

"I will help you," said Ilka. "I know what to do, but I need a couple of days."

"You need a couple of days." Something curious always happened to Ilka's words when Eliza repeated them back to her.

"Meanwhile, Eliza," said Ilka, "please talk to Jenny! Jenny is on her way over to see you. Let Jenny in."

Eliza hung up.

"Maggie," Ilka said to her little girl, "Omama Flora wants you to come and spend the night because I'm going to be busy and grumpy."

"How come?" Maggie asked.

"Because Eliza is really, really sad and I'm going to look for some things that will make her feel better."

Maggie's *How come* was an all-purpose question that didn't mean *What is the cause* so much as *Tell me about things.*

Ilka said "There are some things in some letters that I'm going to look for."

"How come?" Maggie asked.

"You and I are going to Concordance and stay with Jenny and Joe and you can play with Bethy and Teddy."

Ilka had meant—had been wanting—to reread and chronologically order the seven years' worth of letters—his and from a point in time, hers as well. The first plan had been for Ilka to write Leslie at the institute, for him to read her letters, to reply, and destroy them. This, he wrote, he found himself unable to do. Plan B was to read, reply, and return her letters to her. "Let us not destroy," he had written.

The first was a single sheet he had put in her hand on the stair: "And to be friends already, to like each other and know each other well so that loving becomes only another conversation!" The postscript read: "Let's not talk on the telephone except to make arrangements. I for one cannot feel electronically." Then the early notes disguised as office memos.

The letters they had exchanged during the first winter holidays. "Would it be awkward for you if I leveled with my mother? My only hesitation would be her too great interest. Maggie, of course, must not ever be bothered." From the office Leslie wrote: "Tell your mother. Your mother will be shocked and happy for us. I love your mother even if she is bossy and shouts commands from one end of the apartment to the other." Ilka wrote, "You think my mother is bossy?" "Like you, darling." Ilka wrote: "Bossy! Me? Really?" She had liked Leslie, who liked her so much, to tell her things about herself. "Poor Jimmy used to say being married to me was like wearing a perpetually new pair of shoes."

Eliza had written her from home: "Nat has left Nancy and moved in with one of this year's interns, which is not very original of him." Leslie had added, "Nat is a moral lightweight." Ilka replied, "Yes, well, that's what human people do. And he's a good poet." They were embarked on one of their lively three-way quarrels with Leslie and Eliza, as so often, on the same side of the argument. Leslie: "As good a poet as a moral lightweight can be." "Leslie means moral sleazeball," amended Eliza. Leslie's postscript said: "I've sent you, under separate cover, my latest chapter. I'll be glad of your thoughts. Give your mother and Maggie our love." "Love!" There was the word! They had been used to signing off with an easy "Love, Ilka," "Love, Leslie," which, now, at first, both withheld, shy of what it had come so tremendously to signify.

Leslie and Eliza had sent their Christmas card to New York. Ilka waited to respond with what she thought of as her Yom Kippur card, using the Jewish year's end to round up her friends and marvel at all the people she knew in America.

Now Ilka built a tower of books on the floor to clear a surface on which to spread the letters they had written to each other after the week Leslie, Eliza, Ilka, her mother and little Maggie had spent in the Verquières house, and the mistral had settled in for days on end, and Eliza's terrible collapse. Leslie had taken Eliza back to the States. "Because I wanted to spend as much time as possible as close to you as possible, I did not support Eliza," he wrote. Ilka wrote, "Do we have a plan for de-escalation, withdrawal? Shall we pull out our troops? Stop now?" "What! De-escalate? Stop! Who us?" he had written. "So now we know our limits and will stay within them. We will do this right."

Leslie had not discouraged Ilka when she was offered a fine job in New York. "And it will give you greater liberty to meet some-one who can give you the life I can't," he wrote her. "When that happens tell me and I will know how to take myself out of your way." "Preserve me!" Ilka had retorted.

Both Leslie and Ilka had jobs that required travel. They had made their arrangements. Ilka wrote: "The spirit moves me to write and tell you that I love you and that you can take the limousine to the Sheraton at A street and X Avenue. (USS is cheaper and they have shuttle service but not on Sunday mornings.) The room is reserved in your name. If you do the wine I'll bring the fruit, the cheese and the bread." "Now there is an actual date," he wrote, "you begin to be solid again." Ilka wrote: "Until we are in the same room, this undifferentiated longing fixes on some one memory like the last time, at my place, when you stood up from where you were sit-ting and came and sat in the chair close to me." Concordance was in the habit of renting Ilka's spare room when institute people came to New York on institute business. When in town Leslie was known to be staying there.

These were the years Leslie and Ilka made love, talked love, and wrote to each other. The sequence of the letters was not easy to establish for it had never occurred to either to date this or that moment. Ilka might write, "Friday midnight after the morning you left." Leslie wrote: "Monday. Weren't we wonderful!" She was able to arrange the letters by the paper they were written on. Leslie had used Concordance letterhead except for one two-month period—he must have come across a batch of stationery brought over from Oxford. Ilka got through her linen birthday paper in two weeks. Was it a secondary sexual characteristic that he made himself beautifully clear on a single sheet while she required pages and pages to trace her own meaning to its source in some earlier exchange between them, or something read, heard, seen—narratives that led back to some mini-trauma or to the big old one in her childhood Vienna? "Your last good letter," and "your lovely letter," he wrote her. Ilka marveled at his passionate courtesy. "I imagine you hefting yet another fat envelope and I wonder if it's a chore or a thrill." She admired Leslie's reticence, even as she sought to undermine it. "My urge to tell you is as strong as the urge to touch you!" she wrote. "I feel like writing you the minute you leave whereas you can wait till next Monday!"

"Things are churned up by our deepest loving," he wrote. "Just the usual junk of the unconscious—the lost child revisiting. I'm used to it, but at the time I find it troubling. Hence my discourteous tardiness in writing after we have transcended ourselves. Oh love!" he had written.

Ilka could interface one letter with another to which it must have been the answer: Her, "You talk love to me in words that of all the ways to put it most precisely suit me. I am dazzled by my

luck," had preceded his: "Luck is another word for grace," followed by hers: "I'm dazzled by your word: Grace." Ilka had
found herself adopting his vocabulary: "What blessed fun," she
wrote, "to be allowed to borrow you to love for a while. I feel im-
pregnable for minutes on end. How did I get to be happy! Amazing." "Why are you amazed?" he wrote. "Isn't it normal to love,
to be loved, to be and make happy?" "No. Nature and nurture may
have formed you for graced love, but I feel every love and each
friendship to be a gorgeous accident, an error in my favor and in
danger of correction."

(What in hell had Ilka written in the letter that got into Eliza's
hands? What had Eliza been forced to know?)

The letters Eliza had written to Ilka from Elm Street were
typed and dated and fixed the year: "Maggie going on to high
school! And you wouldn't know Teddy Bernstine. He is a new
and different shape of boy. Bethy is a new shape also, grown
grossly overweight." Leslie had added, "And insufferable. One
has seen this curiosity before: the parents at all times scrupulously
courteous to the child who never addresses them under a shout."
Ilka returned: "Poor Bethy! She shouts because she knows her
parents are sorry for her which frightens her." They were off.
Leslie wrote: "Why 'poor' Bethy! Is there no bad behavior that
you are willing to fault?" ("Yes! *Mine!*" she wrote to him to the institute, meaning him to add "and mine!") Eliza wrote: "You
would make excuses for 'poor' Iago. Who could blame him for
causing the deaths of Cassio, Desdemona, Othello, not to speak of
his own wife. He was passed over for a promotion!" "I've always
thought," replied Ilka, "that Iago was trying to account to himself
for being so terrible." Eliza wrote, "Remind your mother that she
owes me her recipe for cheese straws." Reading this good-natured
argument so many years later, Ilka experienced the void in the
belly that comes when we recognize the movie we are watching:
we have watched it before and know the characters inside the car
are on the road to the accident.

———

Not yet; they had not yet turned the corner. "Even our all-night argument was happiness," Leslie had written Ilka—they had come to be with each other in a LaGuardia motel—"how endlessly we misunderstand each other so that we must go on talking forever, thank god."

Ilka took a piece of paper, took a pen and copied out: "How endlessly we misunderstand each other," suppressing "we must go on talking forever" and "thank god."

"Do you believe in god?" she had asked him. "That's not a good question," he replied, "like the question 'Do you love me?' the answer to which is, 'No, though I did a minute before you asked me and will again the minute after.' I believe there is something eternal outside ourselves, and that I don't know much about it."

Ilka, ensorcelled, had fallen in love with Leslie all over again and again and again.

Ilka had written him from a summer in Portugal: "Maggie smells of saltwater and is a dear, civilized little travel companion. She looks and takes everything in, at least I think she does. She makes it her business that I leave tips. My mother is driving us crazy. What you see as her bossiness, I see as anxiety—for us to be on time, for us to be clean and safe, even the anxiety to be agreeable."

"Your Concordance friends," wrote Leslie, "keep wondering why you have not married again, and I worry." Ilka wrote: "Should I be touched by your care for me or irritated at your taking my mother's tack. Chrissake, Leslie! This is hardly polite of you!" "I beg your pardon," he wrote, "but I thought you understood why this troubles me." Ilka answered: "I'm always surprised that things trouble you. You never let on." "But you know my big, big trouble about Eliza. I'm not going to dump that on you." "Oh dump, darling! Dump! Don't I tell you every thought you don't ask me anything about?" "Wonderful, and wonderful," wrote Leslie, "that I'll know everything you want me to know, whether I want to know it or not, and you won't know anything I don't want you to know, whether you want to know it or not."

This also, leaving out the two wonderfuls, Ilka copied out onto her paper.

Ilka had heard trouble when Leslie made one of his rare phone calls. He was canceling a planned visit to New York.

"What happened to your voice? You don't sound like yourself," said Ilka.

"My voice closes up when I am angry. Eliza had a bad night. She is better now but has asked me to stay with her and that's what I will do. She hasn't often done this to me."

"What has she done to you?"

"Deprived me of you."

"You can hardly blame her! How can you be angry with her for that!"

"I don't know what I can or can't but it's strangling me."

"I shall miss you terribly," said Ilka. "Tell Celie I can put Nat up when he comes to collect his National Book Award because I told him the room was not available."

Leslie said, "I told him the institute would stand him a hotel."

"Well," said Ilka, "he says this time he's left Nancy for good and needs to hole up at my place."

"Nat and I went to hear Mostly Mozart, we went to dinner," Ilka wrote to Leslie and Eliza at Elm Street. "He says that he is finally convinced he is *the* poet." "I am glad you and Nat are showing each other a good time," wrote Leslie, "though I doubt if Nat's contemporaries think of him as 'the' poet." Ilka wrote: "You have committed the eighth venal sin which I have just invented. The eighth venal sin is to misunderstand a friend's irony." Leslie wrote: "Neither Eliza nor I see the irony in your believing Nat is 'the' poet of our times." "Then the two of you have missed two ironies. Mine and Nat's." "If you say so," wrote Leslie, "but why the gleeful enthusiasm with which you hate my latest chapter?" "Glee! Enthusiasm! I disagree with what you say. Haven't we always enjoyed our disagreements?" Leslie wrote: "Your poor opinion of my writing is creating a strain between us."

In copying this Ilka changed it to: "Your poor opinion of my writing has always been a strain between us."

Ilka had quoted Leslie back to himself: "You once wrote me, 'How endlessly we misunderstand each other so that we must go on talking forever, thank God.'" "Our misunderstandings," he had replied, "which used to be an intellectual pleasure and excitement turn into weapons when you use your absolutes against me."

Ilka copied out, "Our misunderstandings turn into weapons."

Ilka had written Leslie, "You, with your mercilessly principled judgment on Bethy, your dismissal of Nat, are the absolutist. My natural mode resembles a game of tennis in which I cover both sides of the court. I serve myself an idea, jump over the net to return it to myself, jump back to be ready to return the return. You know what? I think it's my doubts that swell my noise." "Universal doubt is the recipe for nihilism. You are a nihilist. Your absolutism is to be at war with every and any belief, with belief as such."

Ilka copied this onto the paper.

"No," she had answered, "I'm at war with true-belief."

He had written and she copied: "You see a true-believer behind every bush. You are the fanatic of the middle. Read your Dante and see the place to which he damns the trimmers who commit themselves to nothing."

There had followed a week when no letter came from the institute, none from Elm Street where Ilka had finally called him.

Leslie said, "The phone is right outside Eliza's bedroom. I will write you." He wrote: "I had hoped that a few peaceful days would permit the chunks that have been floating around in my soul to quit bumping into one another long enough for me to push and tug them into at least an ur-Stonehenge sort of arrangement. But the days have not been peaceful. I had to spend a day in the hospital for tests—everything seems all right, but it meant leaving Eliza alone and in a very fragile state. I worry how she would fare without me. I must pay attention."

Why, at that juncture, hadn't Ilka offered to pull out the troops? Because she did not have the sweet confidence in his refusal. "Leslie," she had asked, "what exactly are we disagreeing *about*?" "I am not as strong as you think me," he had answered, "I'm not able, right now, to manage. Taking myself out of the way now you are beginning, quite rightly, to consider other men, your finding Nat Cohn a pleasing companion—is a monumental, a physical exertion for me, together with my fear that our quarrel will get into bed with us. Let us stop before love becomes polluted and happiness turns out to have been illusion . . ."

Ilka stopped reading to copy out: "Happiness turns out to have been illusion."

". . . Maybe some time in the future—god knows—we can come together again but at this moment my business is to be available to Eliza, which I can hardly imagine managing if, after you and I are no longer lovers, you will not remain my dear friend."

Ilka wrote him back her fable.

A FABLE

Once there was a man who had a wife and a woman whom he loved. The man said to his wife, "Let's go to sea in a boat," and to the woman whom he loved he said, "Come with us." The three set out together. The sea was calm, the sky friendly, and they were happy. Presently the sky darkened, the sea rose up. The man saw that his wife was deathly afraid and he took the woman he loved and threw her overboard saying, "Our happiness was an illusion." The woman went under and came up and held her hand out to the man. He called to her, "I do this for your sake so that if a boat passes with a man in it without a wife, he may pick you up!" The woman went under a second time and came up and held out her hand to the man. He called to her, "I do this so our love won't get polluted!" She went under a third time and the third time she came up and held her hand out to him and he called, "A time may come when I can come back for you!" She went under and came up for the last time and he shook her hand and said, "I hope we shall always be friends."

Ilka and Maggie stayed with the Bernstines. "No, you can't come and see Eliza," Ilka said to the child. "When you're thirty-five years old, I'll tell you a story."

"How come?" asked Maggie.

Jenny Bernstine said, "You kids go out and play in the yard. Take the dog."

Ilka said, "My mistake was to call ahead. It gave Eliza the chance to say, 'Unfortunately I am out of town for the duration.' I'll call again." Ilka dialed Eliza's number and said, "Eliza, I have something here I want to read to you. Listen, Eliza, please. Eliza?" Ilka listened and heard the silence of nobody on the other end. Eliza had hung up. "I'm going over there."

Ilka rang Eliza's front-door bell. She knocked and she knocked. She walked around the house peering in the dining-room win-

dow and saw the piles of papers laid out on the table and over
every surface. The paper looked dusty and dry, beginning to curl
at the corners. Ilka went to the back door and knocked on it. She
looked in the kitchen window. The kitchen table was covered with
papers; there were papers on the counters, papers on the drain
board. Ilka returned to the front of the house, parted the overgrown bushes and looked into the living room. Eliza sat on a
straight chair with her back to the window. Ilka watched her pick
up the water glass half full of white wine, carry it to her lips, sip
and set it down. There were pages of manuscript on the seats of
the two armchairs and the sofa. "Eliza!" Ilka knocked on the window. It was open an inch at the bottom and Ilka tried to push it up.
It was latched on the inside. Kneeling on the ground she was able
to align her mouth with the opening. "Hi, Eliza? Eliza, listen. I
want to read you some things he wrote me. Listen to this: 'How
endlessly we misunderstand each other. Your poor opinion of my
writing has always been a strain between us. Our misunderstandings turn into weapons.' Does that sound hot and heavy to you?"
Eliza got up. Was it Eliza, bent and gray, a hairy crone walking
toward Ilka on the other side of the glass? "You asked me to help
you, Eliza. Listen. He thought that I was bossy. He wrote me, 'You
are a nihilist.' And here: 'Your absolutism is to be at war with every
and any belief, with belief as such. Read your Dante and see the
place to which he damns the trimmers who commit themselves to
nothing.' Eliza, listen! 'Happiness turns out to have been illusion.
And polluted.'" Eliza unlatched the window. She pushed it all the
way down, refastened the latch and walked with an unsteady gait
to the chair with its back to the window. She sat down. She picked
up the glass and unhurriedly brought it to her lips.

"I don't know that she heard anything I was saying," Ilka reported to the Bernstines. "Joe, give me Matsue's number."
"Hello, Matsue. Yes! Ilka. Hello. I'm in Concordance for a few

days. Yes, thank you. Listen, Matsue, can the reverse bug broadcast some sentences into the living room of a private house? It can! It can't? Why can't it? Why can't you? I don't understand what you are saying." "I don't know a thing he was saying," Ilka told the Bernstines.

Joe said, "The lawyers have drawn up Matsue's contract so that he is prohibited from conducting experiments in Concordance proper."

Jenny brought Ilka a cup of coffee. Joe watched her drink it. Ilka looked out the window into the yard. Poor Bethy stood with her back against the wall watching Maggie and Teddy chase the barking puppy. Ilka said, "This wasn't ever going to do her any good? This was nonsense from the start?"

———

Ilka's mother died. Eliza Shakespeare died. Nat Cohn was dead. The Jewish year turned, and Ilka called Maggie, who was a grown-up with a life. "Remember when you put all my friends on my computer for me? Well, it's crashed! I don't know anybody's address and can't send out my Yom Kippur cards! The only people I still know in Concordance are Celie, the receptionist, remember her? And Yvette. And Mrs. Boots, the cleaning woman. I doubt if anybody ever knew her address. Alpha and Alfred are retired near Santa Fe, I think. Nancy Cohn has moved god knows where. The Bernstines are in France. I've lost my friends—all the people I know in America."

"Oh, Mom! You've never in your life thrown away a piece of paper that had words written on it. When I transcribed your addresses onto the computer did you toss out your old address book?"

"I can't imagine throwing an address book out."

"Look for your old address book and you'll find people who will know where people are."

"I do love you."

"Yes, dear."

"You're wonderfully full of common sense, which is beautiful."

"O.K., Mom."

It was while she was looking for her old address book that Ilka came once again across the old correspondence. "Since the day your letter ran me over," she had written, "I've learned to keep my mouth neutral while we shop for Maggie's back-to-school jeans and shirts and shoes. How could you put an end to love by letter? Why not face to face?" "I was cowardly," he had answered.

There followed a series of his letters written from Elm Street, dated, heartbreakingly friendly—Leslie attempting to stuff the years of passion back into the mold that had contained their easy, early friendship. Concordance chat: Cassandra had met her appropriate end. She had gone barking after a woman on a bicycle whom she must have suspected of some crime or misdemeanor. She got run over by an oncoming car—not the cyclist. Cassandra. The Bernstines have got Teddy a puppy and hope it will be less judgmental. We had dinner at the Stones', who send their love. Nat Cohn tells me he is coming to New York to stay with you. Please write us at Elm Street."

But Ilka continued to write him at the institute, had written reams, apologizing for the lined yellow foolscap and the pencil which could be erased, could modify, expand, interpolate to get the thing said right, clarified, explained, explained, and explained.

To Elm Street Ilka had written: "Nat was in town and has, I'm happy to say, gone home again. The problem is not Nat's morals but his conversation, which, like himself, has grown fat."

By return mail Leslie wrote, "I have reread your old letter about Nat saying he was 'the' poet and cannot understand how I missed the irony. Eliza is in pretty good shape and thinks of coming with me to next month's New York meeting if you can put us up."

As the date approached Eliza had become less and less disposed to travel. Leslie came by himself but stayed at the little hotel around the corner from Ilka. He took her to dinner at one of their favorite restaurants. She said, "I've come across a Göthe poem called 'Parting' which says, *Und doch welch Glück geliebt zu werden! Und lieben, Götter, welch ein Glück!*"

"Will you translate it for me?"

"*Glück* can mean either *luck* or *joy*. *Und doch* means *and yet*, but what I think he's saying is, *in spite of all the crap*. So: 'In spite of everything, the sheer luck of being loved. And, oh ye gods, the joy of loving.'"

Leslie said, "Maggie is at your mother's for the night?"

"Yes."

"Can we go to your place?"

There followed years—Ilka remembered them as the halcyon years in which she had written to him at the institute and he returned her letters enclosed in his answering letters, arranging where to meet. They wrote about joy, they talked about their luck. Where had they been and what could she have said across the table, at dinner, that caused him to ask, "Do you expect me to decamp again?" She had had to take time to think and had answered, "I don't."

And this from Leslie, the following May: "Eliza says you and I ought to go to Greece." "What does that mean?" Ilka had written him back. Leslie wrote: "She remembers our sitting around after your wedding, you and Jimmy wanting a honeymoon in Greece. You got pregnant and then Jimmy died, so you never got to go. I have never been to Greece and I want to go. Eliza does not want to go. She suggests we go together." "I don't understand," wrote Ilka. "A gift horse," wrote Leslie. "She's either crazy or incomparably generous," wrote Ilka. "Yes," wrote Leslie. "Can it be that in another week you and I will be in Athens together? Can we be so elevated? Oh love oh love oh love!" he had written, fifteen years ago. Was it really so? Had this been?

Maggie stayed with her grandmother. Ilka took the opportunity to go on a Hellenic cruise; Leslie, who did not choose to take off more than a week, would meet her in Athens.

In those days the public was still permitted to climb up the promontory and stand and walk among glories, fallen marble, upstanding columns, compared with which other things are only pretty; this is what they said to each other. In their room in the hotel at the foot of the Parthenon they loved each other. It was in the air on the flight home to America that Leslie died. Back in New York Ilka fell into an exhausted sleep. She felt the mattress lowering as under the weight of a body sitting down on the edge. The bed shook with friendly laughter: Leslie on the edge of Ilka's bed laughing at her. Ilka went on sleeping.

"Did you find your address book?" Maggie called to ask her mother.

"No," said Ilka. "I don't know anybody's address. Maggie, oh, I don't even know where Bethy is." Ilka wept. She wept and wept.

Printed in the USA
CPSIA information can be obtained
at www.ICGtesting.com
JSHW020528130923
48424JS00001B/2